The
Pretty Pink Shroud

The
Pretty Pink Shroud

E. X. FERRARS

PUBLISHED FOR THE CRIME CLUB BY

DOUBLEDAY & COMPANY, INC.

GARDEN CITY, NEW YORK

1977

c.1

M

All of the characters in this book
are fictitious, and any resemblance
to actual persons, living or dead,
is purely coincidental.

Library of Congress Cataloging in Publication Data

Ferrars, E. X.
The Pretty Pink Shroud.

I. Title.
PZ3.B81742Pr3   [PR6003.R458]   823'.9'12
PZ3.B81742PR3   [PR6003.R458]   823'.9'12
ISBN: 0-385-12827-4
Library of Congress Catalog Card Number 76–56288

BL

The
Pretty Pink Shroud

CHAPTER 1

Ingrid woke with a sense of depression. It took all the brightness out of the early-morning sunshine that streamed across her bed. But why was she depressed? That somewhat important fact eluded her. Then she remembered. The house. The house agent's particulars had sounded so promising that for once she and Martin had been really hopeful. But when they saw the place they had both agreed that even if they spent a lot of money on it (and where was that money to come from?), it would still be horrible. Pokey, dark rooms, no cupboards, a kitchen with fittings that dated back to the beginning of the century, a faint smell of dry rot, and a garden too small to be interesting but big enough to be a nuisance and overlooked by all the houses round it.

In its way it had been as bad as the house that they had looked at last, which had been very recently built and had all modern conveniences, but in character was not unlike a rabbit hutch, standing cheek by jowl with identical houses on either side of it.

But if she and Martin went on like this, if they insisted on being perfectionists, would they ever get married?

The irony of the situation was that Ingrid was ready to move into Martin's bed-sitting-room today, tomorrow, or any day that he chose to name. It was he who insisted coolly, inflexibly, that they must begin as they meant to go on. The clarity with which he seemed to see the importance of this sometimes almost broke Ingrid's spirit. She loved him and wanted him on any terms, so why did he have to be so intransigent?

Her bedroom door opened and her mother came in, carrying a cup of tea.

"I've just made this," she said. "I thought you might like some."

Ingrid looked at her watch.

"But it's only a quarter to seven. What on earth are you doing, up so early?"

"I haven't been able to sleep," Ruth Winter answered. "I've had a horrible night. It's flu, I'm afraid, as I thought it was yesterday evening, though I hoped perhaps I'd sleep it off. But it's only gone on getting worse. I've a headache and a throat like sandpaper and I feel as if I've got a temperature."

"Have you taken it?" Ingrid asked.

"I can't remember what I've done with the thermometer."

The house was full of things that Ruth Winter had put she could not remember where.

Ingrid sat up in bed and took the cup of tea from her mother.

"Why didn't you call me?" she asked. "You ought to have stayed in bed. I'd have got the tea."

"I was so restless, I wanted to get up."

Ruth lingered at the bedside. She was a small woman of fifty-five with a soft fluff of grey hair curling round her small, fine-featured face, which was wrinkled a little too deeply for her age, but which had a flashing liveliness in the big dark eyes when her interest in anything was kindled. Today her eyes were too bright and there were patches of red on her normally pale cheeks. She was wearing her old blue woollen dressing-gown, pulled in tightly round her narrow waist with a frayed cord.

She added, frowning, "Ingrid, I'm worried."

"Let's phone Dr. McCallum, then," Ingrid said. "And as soon as the shops open I'll go out and get a thermometer. And now go back to bed, please. I'll get breakfast."

"No, I don't mean that," Ruth said. "This is just flu. It doesn't matter. If we phone old McCallum he'll only fill me full of pills and I'll feel worse than ever. No, it's about Ronald."

Ronald Starkey was Ruth's lodger. She only occasionally took a lodger and then only if she had taken a fancy to him, and this she had instantly done to the man who had been occupying the big front bedroom on the first floor for the last six weeks, and who on his first day in the house had stopped being Mr. Starkey and become Ronald.

"What's wrong with him?" Ingrid asked.

"He isn't there. I noticed his door was open as I came up and I looked in to ask him if he'd like a cup of tea and he isn't there."

"D'you mean he's gone out early?"

"I don't think he ever came home last night. His bed hasn't been slept in."

"Then, I suppose he slept in some other bed." Ingrid sipped the hot tea. "He seemed to be having a very good time at the ball last night. I should think he'd have quite a bit of choice about where to end up."

She was speaking of the fancy dress ball that was held once a year for charity by the Pottershill League of Social Service in the great hall of Pottershill's old castle. Ronald Starkey, a small, brittle-looking grasshopper of a man of about thirty-five with a snub-nosed face and an eager smile, had gone to the ball in an old cotton dress that he had borrowed from Ingrid that dated from the days of the miniskirt, short white socks and sandals and with a bow of red ribbon tied to a tuft of his rather long, reddish hair. He had carried a large plastic doll that Ruth had found at the back of what had once been Ingrid's toy cupboard. He had been delighted with his own appearance and had insisted on speaking in a squeaky, little girl's voice. Ruth herself had not gone to the ball because she had not been feeling well. Ingrid had draped herself in a variety of coloured scarves, put on some big hoops of earrings and had hoped to pass as a gypsy. Ronald Starkey had driven her to the castle in his car, but they had soon parted company there and she had been brought home by some other friends.

Martin, of course, had not been there. He had been on duty. Not that anything on earth would have got him into fancy dress even if he had been free that evening.

"What puzzles me," Ruth said, "is that Ronald's car's outside in the usual place, so it looks as if he came home and then went out again."

Her house had no garage and Ronald had to park his car in the street.

"Didn't you hear him come in?" Ingrid asked.

"No, you know how softly he walks. He always creeps about on his toes. And I expect he'd have been extra careful not to disturb us, coming in late. Did you notice if his car was there when you got home?"

"I don't remember."

Ingrid did not remember anything much about the evening. She knew that she had danced until she was exhausted and probably had talked too much and drunk more than she usually did and eaten quantities of tasteless little bits and pieces that waiters in red coats had

kept bringing round on trays, but what had happened to
Ronald Starkey during the evening and whether or not
his car had been standing outside the house when she returned to it were matters to which she had given no
thought at all.

"Anyway, if his car's there he can't have been in a crash
or anything like that," she said. "I shouldn't worry about
him. I'm sure he can look after himself only too well."

Ruth sighed. "You've never really liked him, have you?"
She liked most people herself and never could understand
why sometimes they did not take to each other. "You
know how helpful he is in the house and he makes me
laugh a lot."

"I just find it difficult to believe half the things he tells
one about himself," Ingrid said. "Why didn't he stay in
New Zealand if he'd such a good job there?"

"He's got a roving disposition," Ruth said. "Besides, he
told me it's important for writers to travel."

"I think the truth is that the dairy farming he says he
was doing was too like hard work. And it happens he's got
a generous brother-in-law here, who I'm quite sure is
helping him out while he twiddles his thumbs."

"*Ex*-brother-in-law," Ruth corrected her.

Her lodger was the brother of the woman who had
been the first wife of an old friend of hers, Edward Guest,
who had retired a year before from the Vice-Chancellorship of the University of Tondolo, the capital of one
of the recently liberated, smaller African countries, the
new name of which she could never remember, and who
had come to live in Pottershill.

"And I'm sure if Edward's lending Ronald money," she
went on, "it's because he believes in him. When Ronald's
book is published he'll pay it all back."

"What book?" Ingrid asked. "Have you ever seen any

signs, when you've been doing his room, that he's writing anything?"

"I suppose he puts the manuscript away out of sight," Ruth said. "He may be self-conscious about it. I believe some people are like that. Jane Austen was, you know. Just think of that. Anyway, what else does he do with himself, up in his room all those hours alone?"

"Sleeps, I shouldn't wonder, till the pubs open."

"Oh, Ingrid . . ."

Ingrid laughed. "Don't take any notice of me. I think I had too much to drink last night. There was a nasty sweet sort of wine cup, and I think it was stronger than it seemed."

"Did you enjoy yourself?"

"Not particularly. I might have if Martin had been there. Now do go back to bed."

"Presently," Ruth said. "Don't worry about me. I'm all right." She started towards the door. But she paused. "I was nearly forgetting. I wanted to ask you if you'd do my stint for me at the Economy Centre this morning. I always do Saturday mornings, but I really don't think I'm up to it today, and I hate to let them down. If you'd go instead of me and just explain about the flu, I'd be awfully grateful."

The Economy Centre was a charity that ran a shop where good secondhand clothes were sold to help feed the starving millions in the less fortunate countries of the world. It was staffed by voluntary workers like Ruth.

"I'll go, if you like, but I shan't be much use," Ingrid said. "I don't know anything about the job."

"There's nothing to it. The others will show you what to do. You may even not be needed, but Saturday mornings are always busy. Thank you, darling, it's just that I don't want them to think I haven't bothered."

Ruth went out, shutting the door behind her.

Ingrid finished her tea and got up. She was taller than her mother but had the same slenderness and delicate bones, the same small waist and narrow hands and feet. Her hair, as Ruth's had once been, was almost black and she wore it hanging heavy and straight to her shoulders. She had a high, rounded forehead and dark, serious eyes. At the age of twenty-four she had taken a degree in sociology at London University, then a Ph.D., and now was looking for a job. But recently she had not been working at this very hard. During a vacation that she had spent with her mother she had met Martin Rhymer, and after taking almost nine months to make up their minds, they had decided to get married. A fearful waste of time all those months sometimes seemed now. Ingrid's earlier experiences of love had been far more headlong. Yet she admitted to herself that there had been an odd, novel sense of security in the caution with which she and Martin had approached one another.

The Economy Centre opened at half past nine. It was in Castle Street, the main artery through the middle of Pottershill. The pavements on the way to it were strewn with russet leaves. The trees in the gardens were mostly tawny or golden, shining luminously against the pale, sharp blue of the October morning sky. Castle Street was a long, narrow street that wound upwards along the spine of a hill to the castle at the top of it. Or what had once been a castle. It had been added to, repaired and restored so often that only one or two of its old towers and a few stretches of wall, built of massive stones and topped with battlements, remained to make it recognisable as what it had once been. It now housed the Town Council offices, the police station, and one or two halls that were used for functions such as the fancy dress ball of the evening before.

In Ruth's bright little red Mini it took Ingrid only five

minutes to reach the Economy Centre. It had two shop windows with a door between them. Both windows displayed good though slightly limp-looking clothes, which included, amongst blouses and skirts and men's suits and some rather outdated evening dresses, an old musquash coat in very good condition and a surprisingly fine Paisley shawl.

May Belcher, a woman whom Ingrid knew slightly, was just unlocking the door when she parked the car down a turning next to the shop. May was the widow of a solicitor in the town, a big, sturdily built woman of about fifty with heavy, handsome features. Her three daughters had all married and left home, and May now had a great deal of surplus energy to devote to her church, good works, and coffee mornings with her friends. She was a shrewd, tough bargainer, and the Economy Centre flourished in her hands.

"Hallo, Ingrid," she said. "What's happened to Ruth?"

"She seems to be developing flu," Ingrid answered, "and really isn't up to coming, so she sent me along instead. I'm sorry, I probably shan't be any use."

"Oh, we'll find something to keep you busy," May said in the deep, carrying voice that was so excellent on platforms. "It's very good of you to come. I'm so sorry Ruth isn't well." She led the way into the shop. "Can you sew? There's a pile of stuff that needs mending. Just easy stuff, split seams to stitch up and buttons to put on and things like that. Or would you sooner try your hand at coping with the customers? Everything's priced and we don't let anyone bid us down, though they sometimes try to. It isn't at all difficult."

"Perhaps I'd better stick to the sewing."

Ingrid had often been in the shop before, though she had never actually worked in it. But sometimes she had helped out by picking up consignments of clothing donated by charitably minded people in the neighbourhood and bringing them to the shop by car. The shop consisted of a biggish room with a counter down one side of it and walls lined with shelves on which carefully folded garments of all descriptions were stacked. Several racks stood side by side in the middle of the room with coats and dresses hanging from them. A door behind the counter led into another room in which newly donated clothing was piled and where the ladies who worked in the shop made themselves coffee.

Ingrid knew that the first thing that happened to all the clothes that were brought here, once they had been sorted out and the really useless things thrown away, was that they were made up into bundles and taken to the cleaner's. Yet it always seemed to her that the place had a distinctive and faintly repulsive smell of old clothes, mingled with the equally repellent one of stale coffee. She sometimes wondered why it was her mother's favourite charity, even though Ruth had assured her that the customers alone, with their idiosyncrasies, made the work fascinating.

In the room at the back of the shop May Belcher supplied Ingrid with a needle and thimble, a variety of coloured cottons and a heap of blouses and dresses that all needed some minor repairs. A few minutes later two other women came in. One was Edith Laker, a spinster who until her retirement had been an almoner in the infirmary, was about sixty, brisk, cheerful and an excellent saleswoman. The other was Clare Sykes, a fair, pallid girl of about Ingrid's age who had recently married a teacher in the local comprehensive school. Before her marriage Clare had worked as a secretary in a big engineering firm, but now, in her desperation at not instantly having a child, was rather unhopefully trying out voluntary work as a defence against the boredom of domesticity.

Edith Laker dealt with the first customer who came in, a farmer's wife who was far from poor but who generally came into the shop about twice a year, spent about twenty pounds and went out with a wardrobe for the coming months that made her probably the best-dressed woman in her circle. As she lived at some distance from the town, it was unlikely that any of her friends would ever have seen her clothes on their original wearers.

Clare Sykes came into the room behind the shop and started making instant coffee.

"I saw you at the ball last night," she said to Ingrid in her thin, rather nasal voice. "That was a fabulous costume you were wearing."

"So was yours," Ingrid said, though the truth was that she could not even remember having seen Clare at the ball. It was always difficult to remember much about her except for the wilting look that she generally wore, but it always seemed important to be nice to her.

"Oh, did you think so?" Clare said, looking very pleased. "I liked it myself. I borrowed it from an Indian lady I know. She showed me how to arrange it. But Harold said I looked silly in it, being so fair. What did you think of his costume?"

Vaguely Ingrid remembered that she had once been introduced to Harold Sykes, but his face was not one that had made any impression on her the evening before.

"Well, actually I didn't think it was nearly as successful as yours," she said.

Clare was pouring boiling water into the mugs that held the powdered coffee.

"Oh, didn't you?" She sounded disappointed. "I did my

best. But perhaps it was out of character. I suppose he doesn't really look like a pirate, even with a patch over one eye. Of course, the loveliest dress there was Lady Guest's. I thought she looked marvellous."

"Oh, yes." Even in the abstracted state of mind that Ingrid had been in the evening before, she had noticed Leila Guest flashing by, exquisitely Edwardian in pink satin, dancing a Viennese waltz with her husband on a floor left empty for them. They had been loudly applauded.

"I should think the dress was real, wouldn't you?" Clare went on. "I mean, a real heirloom, even though it looked as if it had been made for her. What a waist she must have. Imagine being able to get into a dress like that without any tight-lacing. I suppose there must have been plenty of bones in the bodice. You know, I think she's one of the most beautiful women I've ever seen. And she dresses so beautifully too."

May Belcher had overheard some of the conversation. She appeared in the doorway.

"Stephanie Legge is bringing in some clothes of Leila's this morning," she said. "She rang up a few days ago to say she'd some things for us, and Stephanie said she'd pick them up and bring them in today. What Leila must spend on clothes! If only I measured a few inches less in all directions I'd buy some of them up myself. They usually look as if they've never been worn."

Edith Laker, who had just got rid of her farmer's wife and was tucking her cheque into the till, burst into song.

"I'm always wearing secondhand clothes,
That's why they call me secondhand Rose . . .

"You know, dears, I think Lady Guest's pushing her luck a bit. I think the crowd of men she keeps around her are beginning to get on Sir Edward's nerves. He doesn't look a happy man."

"I can't remember Edward ever looking happy," May said. "He's had that grim sort of look ever since he came here."

"Well, things have worsened recently, I'm sure of that," Edith said. "Though perhaps he's just bored, being retired. I like it myself. I like the freedom. But then, I was never anyone important. It must be quite difficult for someone like him to sit back and find he's no one in particular."

"He's somehow got himself on to every committee in the place," May said. "He can't feel such a fearful nonentity."

Clare was handing round the mugs of coffee.

"I think he's a wonderfully distinguished-looking man," she said. "I don't think I've ever seen anyone so distinguished-looking."

"Lucky Clare," Edith said. "Her world's just full of wonderfully beautiful and distinguished people."

"But don't you think I'm right?" Clare asked earnestly. "He must have been wonderfully handsome when he was younger."

"He still is, really," May said, "though perhaps he's a bit on the short side. And as a matter of fact, I agree, Leila's being a bit of a fool . . ."

The bell over the street door rang as it opened.

"Oh, customers," she said. "Action stations."

She put down her coffee and turned back into the front shop.

Ingrid went on with her stitching. She was not very good at it, but could just about manage what was required of her. Chatting to the other women in the shop and listening to them dealing with the sometimes curious demands of the customers who came and went, while Clare at intervals made more coffee, the time passed surprisingly quickly.

It was about half past eleven when Stephanie Legge came in with the consignment of clothes that she had collected from the home of the Guests, a spacious bungalow on the edge of the golf course. Stephanie and her husband Andrew, an accountant, lived in the bungalow next door to it. She was a harassed-looking, hurrying, usually breathless woman of about forty, who had perhaps once been pretty in a rather coltish way, but who, as she had grown older, had become merely angular and awkward, while her thin, earnest face, which was deeply tanned by the hours she spent working in her garden, had hardened into lines of anxiety. Only her splendid red hair, which she rolled up carelessly at the back of her head, had not even begun to be tarnished by age. She was wearing a short raincoat over a sagging jersey dress in which, Ingrid felt sure, she could remember Stephanie going about when she herself had still been a schoolgirl.

Stephanie took the pile of clothes that she had brought with her into the back room, and seeing Ingrid, said, "Hallo, I didn't expect to see you here. Is something wrong with Ruth?"

Ingrid explained about Ruth's flu.

"Miserable," Stephanie said. "There's a lot of it about. Make her take care of herself. Now I must rush." She was nearly always in a state of having to rush off somewhere or other. "You can sort out this stuff of Lady Guest's, can't you? It's the usual sort of thing she sends—much too good to be given away, in my opinion."

Edith Laker, who had again been busy with a customer, appeared in the doorway.

"We ought to be grateful," she said. "If you asked her

for a cheque for what those things are worth I'm sure she wouldn't dream of giving it to you."

"In other words, it's just her extravagance with clothes, not a really charitable feeling at all," Stephanie said. "I can't say why, but for some reason that sickens me. I suppose it's the vanity at the back of it. She ought to have begun to get over that by now. She isn't as young as all that."

"She can't be much more than thirty and she *is* so beautiful," Clare said with a sigh. Her gaze dwelt hungrily on the clothes that Stephanie had brought in. "I think she and Sir Edward make a wonderful couple, both of them so good-looking and so sort of, well, dignified. Will you have some coffee, Mrs. Legge?"

"No, thank you, Clare, I really must rush. I want to get to my butcher's before they close. Goodbye, everyone."

Stephanie whisked out of the shop.

Edith laughed. "She doesn't love her neighbour, does she? Poor Stephanie, one thing we can be sure of is that we'll never get any clothes from her. She wears everything she owns until it drops off her. Not that I don't do the same, but I'm twenty years older than she is, and she's really got a very nice figure and could make something of herself if she wanted."

"Perhaps Mr. Legge doesn't allow her enough money for it," Clare suggested, as if she were speaking from experience of husbands. She put down her mug of coffee and began to finger the topmost garment in the pile on the table. "This is a lovely cardigan. Such a lovely shade of red. And a skirt to match. And look at this heavenly trouser suit. Actually, one can't help wondering why Lady Guest gives things like this away."

"Boredom," Edith said. "Having to buy something new gives her an excuse for a trip to London, then she never has any real need to wear what she's bought in a place like Pottershill and it hangs in her wardrobe till she's sick of the sight of it and she gives it away. A town like this must be very discouraging to a woman who likes to dress well."

"I suppose when she was in Africa she needed lots of lovely clothes for parties and things," Clare said. "It must seem very dull here after the life she was used to."

"But at least she can sleep in her bed without being afraid of having her throat cut." May Belcher came in from the front shop, which was empty at the moment, and stood watching as Clare shook out each garment, studied it, looking wistful, folded it again and put it on one side, ready for the cleaner's. "Anyway, she was only Edward's secretary. She can't have had all that much money for clothes or anything else till they got married." She turned to Ingrid with a smile. "What a dreadful lot of old gossips you must be thinking us, Ingrid. I expect you disapprove of us terribly."

Ingrid returned the smile. "Mother warned me. She said I'd find it educational."

"Actually I like Leila," May went on, "and I'm rather sorry for her. I don't think she realised when she married what it was going to mean, giving up the travelling around the earth that she was used to, and all the different jobs she could get because she was so competent, and keeping on seeing new faces."

"My God, my God, look at that!" Clare suddenly shrieked.

The three others in the room all started violently. They looked with astonishment at where Clare was pointing. It was at the last item in the pile of clothes on the table. She was looking at it with horrified fascination.

"It's that gorgeous dress she wore at the ball last night,"

she wailed. "I'm sure it is. And it's real Edwardian, not a fancy dress at all. It must be precious. I'm sure it's worth an immense amount. Oh, how can she give it away? How can she think of it?"

A pink satin dress lay in a crumpled heap on the table. It had been far less carefully folded than the other things that Stephanie Legge had brought in. Clare picked it up gingerly by the shoulder seams and, with a grave look of reverence on her face, lifted it gently and shook it out. Towards the hem it swirled out, giving it the look of an inverted arum lily. It was a low-necked dress brocaded with small ivory speckles that had almost the appearance of snowflakes. The sleeves were short and made of finely pleated ivory chiffon. The neckline was edged with chiffon which spilled over and cascaded to the waistline. There was a look of immense luxury about the dress, of a time when wealth and style meant something. With a bashful half-smile, showing that the gesture was more than she could resist, Clare suddenly draped the dress against her own thin body.

The next moment she had flung it from her onto the floor and was screaming. Her face was a sickly white.

Starting up, expecting to see at least a dead mouse fall out from amongst the frills and folds, Ingrid let the blouse that she was mending slide to the floor. However, there was no mouse to be seen. Not even a spider. But the back of the bodice of the dress, stiffened with bones, had a big, dark-reddish stain on it. In the middle of the stain there was a round hole.

Clare had her hands pressed over her eyes. She was swaying slightly.

"It's blood and I can't stand the sight of blood!" she screamed. "I think I'm going to faint."

"What nonsense—how can it be blood?" May Belcher

bent over the dress, looking at it intently but holding her hands behind her as if to stop herself touching it. "Pull yourself together, Clare. Something got spilled on the dress after Leila took it off and ruined it, and that's why she's sent it to us."

"I must say," Edith Laker said, "it looks remarkably like blood to me."

"And that tear in the middle, it's a bullet hole, I'm sure it is!" Clare cried.

"What nonsense!" May repeated, though her voice sounded less positive than before. "I'm surprised at you, Clare. We all know you're hysterical, but still . . ."

Not screaming this time, but speaking in a hoarse, shaky whisper, Clare said, "I tell you it's blood." She had dropped her hands from her eyes but was being careful not to look at the dress. "What else could it be? Tell me anything else it could be. Tell me anything else it looks like."

"Coffee," May suggested without much conviction.

"A coffee stain wouldn't have got thick and stiff like that," Edith said. She showed less feeling than the others. Perhaps her years in the infirmary had made bloodstains, even with what might be a bullet hole in the middle of them, a more or less everyday affair. "Soup or gravy, perhaps—but down the back of a dress, that's a funny place to spill it."

"She'd taken it off," May said again. "I expect she was longing to get out of all that whalebone, it must have been killing her. And she just dropped the dress somewhere and warmed up some soup, or it might have been some chocolate or a hot drink for her and Edward before going to bed, and something jogged her hand, and— and—" Her voice faltered. "And that hole could have been made by a cigarette end, couldn't it? If she was very sleepy and just let one drop . . ."

"The question is, what are we going to do about it now?" Edith asked. In any crisis she would always be the one to ask the question. "Do we send it along to the cleaner's with all the other things and pretend we never noticed anything?"

"Oh no, we must call the police!" Clare cried. "Immediately. Please, Mrs. Belcher, you do it. Do it now."

"And tell them about some spilled soup?" May gave an uneasy titter, quite unlike her usual hearty laugh. She stood upright, backing a little away from the dress. "I think the first thing we ought to do is to ring up Leila herself and ask her what happened."

"Yes, of course," Edith agreed. "Will you do it, May? You know her better than the rest of us."

"All right." May sounded brisker, more like her usual self. "There'll be some quite simple explanation. We're being rather silly, aren't we, getting excited? All except Ingrid. She's very quiet. What do you think about it, Ingrid?"

Ingrid sat down, picked up the blouse that had fallen to the floor and started stitching again. She thought of how interesting her mother had said the Economy Centre could be, but this was more than she had been prepared for.

"I'm sorry, I honestly don't know," she said.

"I'm sure the first thing to do is to telephone Lady Guest, in case she never meant to put the dress in with the other things," Edith said. "I should think Clare's right, it's quite valuable, and if it was cleaned and somebody clever repaired it, it might still be worth quite a lot."

"That's true, of course," May said. "It's very odd really, sending it to us at all. Perhaps she wasn't, well, altogether sober when she put it in with the other things. That wine cup was really quite potent. All right, I'll ring up and see what she has to say."

She turned to the telephone, picked up the directory that lay beside it, leafed through it for the Guests' number and dialled.

At the other end the telephone was lifted immediately, as if someone had been inside it.

"Edward?" May said. "This is May Belcher. How are you? A wonderful evening last night, wasn't it? Wherever did Leila get that beautiful dress? She looked marvellous in it . . . Oh, your mother's . . . Well, I think it's beautiful. And your own costume, so amazingly simple and ingenious, just ordinary evening dress with a tarboosh and that magnificent star—you manged to look just like an ambassador from one of those Arab places. Is Leila in now, Edward? Can I speak to her? . . . Oh . . . Oh, that's a pity. Something's come up I want to ask her about. When d'you think she'll be back? . . . I see . . . Oh no, don't trouble, I'll ring again later . . . Yes, thank you. Goodbye."

She put the telephone down.

"Leila's out," she said. "He doesn't know when she'll be back."

"Of course she's out," Clare hissed, "and she'll be out next time you ring and the time after. Don't you understand, she's dead?"

"Be quiet, Clare!" Edith said sharply. "The next thing to do, I think, is to ring Stephanie. Ask her if, well, if there was anything peculiar about things when she collected these clothes from Lady Guest this morning. It must have been this morning, as she was wearing the dress last night. I'll do it, if you like."

She reached for the directory and started looking for the Legges' telephone number.

But Stephanie Legge had not yet reached home after

her shopping, so Edith was told by the Legges' daughter, Sandra. Edith put the telephone down.

"Sandra says Stephanie ought to be home anytime now," she said. "But meanwhile, I wonder—I really do wonder—if we oughtn't to get in touch with the police. I don't like the thought of doing it. It seems to me just possible, you know, that we're the victims of a rather gruesome practical joke. Not that I can see Sir Edward as a practical joker, or Lady Guest either, for that matter. But if someone else got hold of the dress . . . Oh, I don't know quite what I mean, but it seems to make more sense than somebody shooting a person, then sending the dress she was wearing to us. That would be a quite mad thing to do, wouldn't it?"

"There are far more mad people about than you'd ever imagine," Clare said sombrely. "Alcoholics and drug addicts and women who steal other people's babies and men who batter their wives and rapists and terrorists who kidnap perfectly innocent people and—"

"Stop!" May commanded. "I don't know where you got your imagination from, Clare. You look so harmless, but you've a most morbid mind. Now I've thought what we ought to do. It's perfectly obvious, once you think of it. We won't go to the police officially, just in case, as Edith said, we've merely had a nasty practical joke played on us. But we'll ask Ingrid to tell the whole story to that nice detective she's engaged to and see what he thinks about it. Meanwhile, of course, we'll telephone Leila and Stephanie again, but in case they can't tell us anything that explains the situation, we'll ask Ingrid to get what advice she can from Detective Inspector Rhymer."

CHAPTER 2

Ingrid remembered to buy a thermometer on her way home. She also bought a cold roast chicken, some frozen peas and some tomatoes, in case her mother, whom she expected to find in bed, had not bought in enough food for the weekend. But Ruth was not in bed. Still in her dressing-gown, she was pottering about the old-fashioned basement kitchen of her small Victorian house, making some macaroni cheese for lunch. She looked flushed and ill.

Ingrid made her sit down and submit to having her temperature taken. It was a hundred and one. As soon as this had been ascertained, Ruth returned to grating cheese.

"Oh, why do you have to be so stubborn?" Ingrid asked, exasperated. "Why won't you go back to bed? I'll go up and switch on your blanket now, then bring you up some lunch presently. Do please go."

"No, no, a hundred and one doesn't mean anything much," Ruth said. "And I'm so worried about Ronald, I don't seem able to settle down. It *is* odd, don't you think, not letting us know about what he's doing? And I've just thought of something, Ingrid. I can't go outside myself in my dressing-gown, but would you go outside for me and see if he's left his keys in the car? If he wasn't too sober when he got home last night and didn't know quite what he was doing, he might have forgotten them, and I shouldn't like to have the car stolen while he's away."

"All right," Ingrid said and went out to where Ronald Starkey's car was parked in front of the house.

In a minute she returned, bringing not only the keys of the car, but her cotton dress, the red hair ribbon that he had worn, and her old plastic doll. She put them down on the table.

"You were right about the keys, and look at this," she said. "It was all jumbled up on the back seat of the car."

Lines of worry appeared on Ruth's forehead.

"So he must have come in, even though I didn't hear him, and changed and gone out again. And I suppose he'll walk in sooner or later, or whoever he went away with will drive him back. But why didn't he just leave the costume in his room? What was the point of bundling it into his car?"

"That's two fancy dresses turned up in rather odd places this morning," Ingrid said.

Ruth asked her what she meant, and Ingrid told her how Leila Guest's ball dress had turned up in the Economy Centre with what might be bloodstains and a bullet hole in the bodice.

Once Ruth understood what had happened, she started shaking her head as if to make it clear that she was not going to be taken in by a story like that.

"That's quite preposterous," she said. "It must have been a practical joke. I mean to say, Leila . . . Edward . . . Can you imagine it?"

"You don't believe he could possibly shoot her, not in any circumstances?" Ingrid inquired with irony.

"My dear, I've sometimes wondered why he hasn't done it already," Ruth answered. "Much as I like her, some of her whims really do go a bit far. Edward's talked to me once or twice about her extravagance. He's the most generous of men, but he's sometimes really upset by the things she does. Of course, he's got his mother's money besides his pension, but he isn't what you'd call a really rich man and Leila doesn't seem to realise it. Oh dear, I do wish this hadn't happened just now of all times. I'd go out to see them this afternoon to find out what it's all really about, before people start building it up into a choice bit of scandal, if only I hadn't got this wretched disease, but it wouldn't be any kindness to them to visit them while I'm so obviously infectious."

"With a temperature of a hundred and one you aren't going anywhere," Ingrid said.

She knew that Edward Guest sometimes confided in her mother about the failings of his beautiful wife, though Ingrid found it hard to envisage him confiding in anyone about anything so personal. He had always seemed to her, for all his charm, to be as reserved a person as she had ever encountered. However, he happened to have been at school and then at Oxford with Ruth's husband and had been best man at their wedding. Not long after it he had gone as an associate professor to the United States, then to a chair in Canada, then had returned to England to the new University of Worcester, where he had made his mark in university administration and achieved distinction in national advisory work. After that, he had gone to the Vice-Chancellorship of the University of Tondolo. However, although he had spent most of his life abroad and sometimes for years on end had seen nothing of the Winters, he had never entirely lost touch with them. When Arnold Winter, a not very successful architect in a Pottershill firm, had died suddenly of a heart attack, so long ago that Ingrid could hardly remember him, Edward Guest had appeared in Pottershill and helped Ruth with friendship and practical advice.

It had been at that time that she had become friends with Edward's first wife, Caroline, Ronald Starkey's sister, who had died two years ago. Ingrid knew that her mother had been surprised when Edward had married again so soon afterwards, for she had always spoken of his first marriage as something remarkable for its intense devotion, but when he had decided on his retirement to come and live in Pottershill, she had done her best to make his new wife welcome. So when from time to time it appeared that it came over this rather remote and formidable man that he must confide in someone about the fact that his second marriage had not turned out too well, it seemed only natural that it should be to Ruth that he turned.

"They wanted me—Mrs. Belcher and the others—to talk to Martin about the dress," Ingrid said, "but I don't want to."

"Why not?" Ruth asked. "It seems to me a very good idea."

"I don't know, it doesn't seem fair somehow. It's like asking a doctor to give you medical advice when you meet at a party."

"Oh no, that's quite different. For one thing, you aren't meeting at a party, you happen to be engaged to him. And for another, the police rely all the time on little bits of information they pick up unofficially, don't they? That's what one's always told. Perhaps it'll even turn out useful to Martin if you tell him what's happened. Anyway, there couldn't possibly be any harm in telling him, whether or not he decides to do anything about it. What time is he coming in this evening?"

"About six, I think, if he can get away."

"I wonder if Ronald will have got back by then. If he hasn't, we could ask Martin what to do about that too."

"Why, are you afraid he's been kidnapped?" Ingrid asked. "If he has, I can't think of anyone who'll pay a ransom."

Ruth gave a sad shake of her head. "I can't make out why you're so unfair to him. You never say a nice thing about him. I've always found him very pleasant and considerate."

"So are a lot of con men, aren't they? I believe they make excellent husbands." Ingrid turned to the door. "Since you won't go to bed, shall I get you a drink?"

"Thank you, that would be lovely. But you know . . ." Ruth prodded the plastic doll. "There *is* something funny about this, perhaps as funny as about Leila's ball dress. Just think what Ronald must have done. He drove home in his car after the dance, wearing this old dress of yours, crept upstairs without waking anybody, changed into normal clothes, went downstairs again, taking the dress and things with him, put them into the car, then either walked off or was driven off by someone who was waiting for him, and he hasn't come back or let us know what's happened to him."

"Perhaps he didn't come into the house at all," Ingrid said. "Perhaps he simply walked off stark naked and got arrested for indecent exposure and is being kept in gaol somewhere."

"Do please be sensible."

"But I really do think there isn't anything specially peculiar about any of it. You're just a chronic worrier."

"No, I think it *is* peculiar that he put these things in the car," Ruth insisted.

"Sheer absent-mindedness. Now wait a minute, I'll get that drink."

Ingrid went up the stairs from the basement, collected a bottle of sherry and two glasses from the living room and brought them back to the kitchen.

Sipping her drink, she went on, "You really want me to tell Martin about Lady Guest's dress?"

"Yes, I think you should," Ruth answered. "He's so wonderfully practical."

"All right, if you want me to."

"And there's something else I'd like you to do too—only you did my shift at the Economy Centre this morning and I don't like to keep on asking for things. I'd do it myself if it weren't for this flu."

"I know, you want me to go and see the Guests," Ingrid said before Ruth could finish. "Isn't that it?"

"It is, as a matter of fact."

"It won't be the same as your going. They hardly know me."

"But it's all right, they like you. Edward's told me so."

"Exactly what am I supposed to say to them?"

"Just tell them what you told me about the dress, and—oh, what I want you to do, I suppose, is just make sure that they're both all right."

"You *are* in a worrying mood this morning," Ingrid said. "I suppose it's the flu."

"Perhaps it is."

"Well, I'll go if you'll promise to go to bed and stay there. Is that a deal?"

Ruth smiled and answered, "Thank you, darling."

As soon as they had had their lunch and Ingrid had made sure that Ruth kept her side of the bargain and really did go to bed, she set off in the Mini for the Guests' house, the bungalow on the edge of the golf course. It had been the golf course, she had been told, that had made the Guests decide on settling in Pottershill. Leila was only a mildly enthusiastic and not very competent player, but Edward could hardly ever be persuaded to let a day go by without going out by himself, if with no one else, for a practice round in the morning. It had kept his figure slim and his stomach flat and his step amazingly light for a man of sixty-one. His hair had gone grey and his face was finely wrinkled, but his spine was as straight as it had ever been. He was of medium height and neat and quick in all his movements. In a dark, sharp-featured, hawk-faced way, he was very handsome. Last night, in evening dress and a tarboosh and with a big tinsel star on a ribbon across his chest, he had looked, as Clare Sykes had said, extremely distinguished.

When Ingrid rang the bell of the bungalow and he came to the door to answer it, he was in a tweed jacket, well-pressed slacks and brown shoes that glowed with polishing. Yet it seemed to Ingrid that he looked less trim than usual. For a moment she could not make out what there was about him that gave her this impression, then she decided that it was mainly that his brown eyes, under his rather bushy dark eyebrows, were bloodshot and that his eyelids were puffy. There was something unusually sagging too about his cheeks. Of course, he had been up late the night before, she remembered, and perhaps at sixty-one that left its scars.

He looked at her blankly for a moment, almost as if he did not recognise her, then said, "Ah, Ingrid."

She thought, from the way he stayed planted in the doorway, that he was not going to ask her in, but then, as if making an effort to recollect what it was right to do when one was called on unexpectedly by a young woman whom one hardly knew, he stood aside and said, "How very nice to see you, Ingrid. Come in. Are you collecting for something? Poppy day? No, it's too early for that. But it's the kind of thing that so many of our more attractive visitors turn out to be doing. Do come in. Can I get you some tea? Some coffee? How's your mother? I'm so sorry she didn't come to our ball last night, but she's never much cared for that sort of thing, has she? But I saw you there. Your costume was charming. Was your fiancé there? Leila and I want so much to meet him, but no doubt he had other, more important things to attend to. You and he must come to dinner with us one evening— you and he and Ruth . . ."

He had ushered Ingrid into the big drawing room of the bungalow and was standing in the middle of it, vaguely talking, as if he did not know how to stop. It was so unlike his usual incisive manner that Ingrid felt puzzled and embarrassed. She noticed that there was a half-empty glass of whisky on the grand piano and wondered if the trouble was that at three in the afternoon he was more than a little drunk.

The piano stood near to the picture window that took up nearly the whole of one wall and overlooked the golf course. The walls of the room were white, the curtains deep blue and the floor of polished hardwood, with a few good rugs scattered here and there. There was not much furniture in the room, but what there was—a pretty Regency writing table, a glass-fronted cabinet full of fine china, a sofa-table, some armchairs—was all graceful and pleasing. It was a cool-looking, dignified room, but Ingrid sometimes wondered which of the Guests played the piano. She had never heard either of them touch it.

"Some coffee," Edward Guest said again. "Do let me make you some coffee. I was just going to make some for myself. You'll join me, won't you? You've had lunch, I expect, but perhaps some biscuits . . . I've only just finished lunch myself, just bread and cheese. Leila's out and I couldn't be bothered to get myself anything else. We had breakfast very late, of course, because of getting home so late last night, and I'm afraid I don't stand up to that kind of thing as well as I used to. Still, it was a splendid evening, wasn't it? Now wait just a minute."

Before Ingrid could say that she did not want any coffee, he shot out of the room.

It worried Ingrid that obviously he did not want her to stay, yet was so afraid that he might hurt her feelings by letting her see this that he was trying frantically to cover it up with his jerky, uncharacteristic chatter. If she had possessed more poise herself, she thought, she would have known how to extricate herself courteously from the situation, but in fact she felt helpless. It seemed to her that there was nothing for her to do but to sit down and wait.

She looked out of the window. There were no houses to be seen from it, only the smooth green of the golf course, with a thick belt of pines in the distance that hid the suburb that began beyond them. The Legges' bungalow next door was out of sight. The Guests had really been very lucky, she thought, when they came house-hunting, to find such a pleasant spot. It was reasonably near to the centre of the town, with its good train service to London, and yet it was very quiet and secluded.

Her gaze moved from the window back to the piano. There was no music on it, and suddenly it occurred to her that there never had been when she had been in the room. So perhaps the truth was that neither of the Guests had played the instrument. Perhaps it had been Sir Edward's first wife who had been the musician and he treasured the piano out of sentiment.

No one ever spoke very much of Caroline Guest. Her death had been the kind of death to which people are careful not to refer. She had had cancer, then had taken an overdose of barbiturates because she could not face the terrors ahead of her. What had she been like? Ingrid wondered. Anything like her brother Ronald? Had she had anything of his insinuating, sly charm, his often malicious and disturbing wit, which always set Ingrid's teeth on edge, though it pleased and amused Ruth?

Edward Guest returned to the drawing room after a few minutes, carrying a tray with cups and a jug of coffee on it.

"Now, what can I do for you?" he asked as he poured out the coffee and handed a cup to Ingrid. "Though I expect it's Leila you came to see, isn't it? I'm sorry she's gone out and I'm not really sure when she'll be back. She didn't tell me. Can I give her a message for you?"

He sat down facing Ingrid across the long, low fireplace and gave her a curiously tight, empty smile. She had never felt at ease with him although she had always admired him, but today she felt totally at a loss as to how to speak to him.

"It was my mother who wanted me to come with a message for Lady Guest," she said. "Mother isn't well, or she'd have come herself. She's got this flu thing that's going about."

"Oh dear, I'm so sorry," he said. "But I suppose her doctor's given her some antibiotic. There are pills for everything nowadays."

"She won't let me send for him," Ingrid answered. "She isn't actually very easy to look after. But she did let me come here instead of coming herself. It's about a dress that Lady Guest sent to the Economy Centre this morning, the dress she wore last night."

"This morning," he said. "She sent a dress to them this morning?"

His tone surprised Ingrid a little, it was so sharp.

"Yes, Mrs. Legge collected some clothes from her this morning," she said, "and brought them along to the shop. I was there instead of mother, because of her flu, and when we undid the parcel, this dress was there, and—" Suddenly she found that she could not speak about the blood that had perhaps been spilled gravy and the bullet hole that might have been made by a cigarette end. "And it's such a beautiful dress," she went on, "we wondered if perhaps it had got in with the other things by mistake. And when I told my mother about it, she thought I ought to come here and make sure that Lady Guest really meant to send it."

"This morning?" he repeated, as if that were the most important thing that she had said. "She sent that dress this morning?"

Ingrid nodded.

"But that's impossible," he said. "Mrs. Legge collected those things from Leila yesterday."

"She couldn't have," Ingrid said. "Lady Guest wore that dress last night at the ball."

"Yes, yes," he said, "but the other things . . ." Gazing down at his hands, he cracked his knuckles loudly. Then he frowned deeply and angrily, as if they had just played some malignant trick on him. After a moment he began to massage them gently, as if he were trying to pacify them. "The other things—I don't know what they were, but Mrs. Legge called in the afternoon about four o'clock yesterday and I saw Leila give her the bundle myself, and of course that pink dress wasn't in it, because, as you say, she wore it in the evening. So I'm afraid I can't understand what happened. You're sure it's the same dress?"

"Oh yes, I'm sure it is. There couldn't be two like that around, could there?"

He managed another of his unnatural smiles, which seemed only to strain the lines of his firm, straight mouth.

"Then it's very mysterious, isn't it? What do you think could have happened?"

"Do you think," Ingrid asked hesitantly, "Lady Guest could have taken the dress over to Mrs. Legge this morning—I mean, before going out for the day—and asked her to bring it along to the Economy Centre when she brought the other things?"

"No!" he exploded and cracked his knuckles fiercely again. Then, as if he felt it necessary to seem less excitable, he said very quietly, "Apart from anything, she'd have had no right to give the dress away without consulting me. She wouldn't have thought of doing it. It belonged to my mother. She knew how I treasured it."

"Then, I suppose the only thing to do is to wait until Lady Guest comes home and ask her just what happened." Ingrid finished her coffee and stood up. "Would you mind asking her to telephone me when she gets in and let me know if the dress is really to be sold?"

He had not stood up when she did. He was looking down at his hands again, still seeming to be trying to control them by softly massaging them.

"It isn't, it isn't," he said. "Certainly not. The Economy Centre, of all places . . . How fantastic." Then he sprang to his feet. "Forgive me. I'm in a rather muddled state today. These late nights don't agree with me any more. I ought to face the fact, my dancing days are over."

He smiled again with the same unconvincing cordiality as before and they went together to the front door.

As he held it open for her, Ingrid said, "I suppose you haven't seen anything of Ronald Starkey since last night?"

"Ronald?" He gave her a startled stare. "No. Why? Should I have seen him?"

"It's just that he never came home after the dance. We don't know where he's gone. My mother's worried."

He gave a slight shake of his head. "He's a person I gave up worrying about a long time ago. He's quite irresponsible. If it wasn't for the fact that my wife—my first wife, Caroline—was very fond of him, I'd have as little to do with him as I could. I'm very sorry that Ruth got landed with him. Leila can't bear him, and when he turned up here she gave him Ruth's address as a place where he might be able to stay. I didn't like it, but I didn't think he'd stay for more than a few days, I never imagined he'd just stay on and on. But your mother really mustn't concern herself about him. He'll walk in sometime with some very tall story about what he's been doing, and when he does, if I were her, I'd give him notice. I hope she doesn't feel she's got to go on putting up with him because Leila sent him to her. Do tell her not to feel that on any account."

"I think she's really got rather fond of him," Ingrid said.

"That's too bad. I'd be sorry for anyone who was fond of Ronald. He used to exploit poor Caroline in a shameless way. I had to interfere more than once. Still, that's all long ago. I do my best not to be too prejudiced against him. He may grow up someday."

He held out a hand. When Ingrid took it, it felt unexpectedly clammy. They said goodbye to one another and Ingrid returned to the Mini.

By the time she reached home the first faint haze of twilight was dimming the brightness of the autumn afternoon. It had become much colder than it had been in the morning. Winter, she thought, was just around the corner, and allowing herself to daydream for a moment as she let herself into the house, she wondered if she and Martin could somehow find the money for a honeymoon in the Caribbean. Wouldn't that be wonderful? If, that was to say, Martin could get enough leave for a real honeymoon anywhere, which was highly improbable.

Ruth had kept her promise and had stayed in bed. She seemed to be dozing when Ingrid looked into her room, but opened her eyes immediately and asked, "Well, what does she say?"

"About the dress? She wasn't there. She's been out all day." Ingrid sat down on the edge of the bed. "How are you feeling?"

"Oh, not bad. I've taken some aspirins."

"You're sure you don't want me to call McCallum?"

"You'd never get him on a Saturday afternoon, anyway. He'll be out playing golf. No, don't fuss about me. I'm all right. Tell me what you found out."

"It's a funny thing," Ingrid said. "Sir Edward swears Mrs. Legge collected the bundle of clothes from Lady Guest yesterday afternoon. He hasn't the faintest idea how the ball dress could have got in with the other things this morning. And he's sure Lady Guest would never have given the dress away without consulting him, because it was his mother's and means a lot to him."

"What did he say about the stains and the hole in the dress?"

"As a matter of fact, I didn't tell him about them."

"Why not?"

"I'm not sure. It would have sounded so . . . Oh, I don't know. Melodramatic or something. A bit ridiculous. But another funny thing . . ."

"Yes?"

"It was something about Sir Edward himself," Ingrid said. "He was quite different from what he's usually like. I think he must have been terribly upset about something.

You know how cool and composed he usually is. Well, today he talked too much in a jerky, disconnected way and he worked fearfully hard at pretending he was glad to see me when really he couldn't wait for me to leave. He told me it was all because of his having had a late night, but I don't think he even expected me to believe him."

"What do you think, then?" Ruth asked. "That he and Leila have had a quarrel?"

"Perhaps."

"You didn't happen to say anything about Ronald?"

"Yes, I did, and he said don't worry about him, he'll walk in sometime."

Ruth gave a sigh and tugged at the pillows behind her head to settle herself more comfortably. Her eyes had a filmed, drowsy look.

"I suppose he's right, there's no point in worrying," she said. "But you'll tell Martin about it all this evening, won't you? About the dress and the stain and the bullet hole and the funny way the dress turned up this morning and Leila being missing today and Edward being so strange . . ." Her voice died away in a wide yawn. After a moment she went on, "I think I'll have a sleep now. Don't let Martin come in to see me, because I don't want him to catch this beastly bug, but tell him everything, won't you? He's so rational, he sees things so clearly, with such detachment. And give him my love . . ." Her eyelids slid down over her eyes.

Ingrid tiptoed to the window, softly drawing the curtains to shut out what was left of the dim autumn daylight, then quietly left the room and went downstairs to the kitchen, where she began to consider what she would cook for the evening.

There had been a time, not long ago, when she, like

Ruth, had thought Martin extremely rational and detached. Now she did not feel at all sure that he was either. She had discovered that he had what she thought of as all kinds of irrational prejudices, as well as a fear of his own emotions which could make him oddly complicated to deal with. The trouble stemmed, she knew, from his first marriage. He had married very young and after five years his wife had left him. He had been working for a charter airline at the time and his wife had been one of the stewardesses. They had never had a home, but had spent brief, wild spells together in Nairobi or Hongkong, Buenos Aires or Oslo, as things had happened to fall out, meeting with ecstasy and parting all too often with boredom, until the glamour of their lives had worn very thin and his wife one day had not appeared at the appointed place, having decided to settle down in affluence and as much stability as her nature would permit with an Australian grazier.

It had been after that that Martin had joined the police. Ingrid understood that there had been something symbolic about this, that it had been a way of grasping at self-discipline. And when, in his late thirties, he had brought himself to think of marriage again, he had insisted from the first that everything must be the opposite of that first devastating experience. Hence his way of keeping her sometimes almost at arm's length, as if he feared that he might actually be rejected if he came too close to her.

He was a tall man, wide-shouldered, spare, with a long, narrow face and a sharply pointed chin, pale-blue eyes and rough, sandy-coloured hair. There was nothing remarkable about his features, except that his long, narrow nose was slightly crooked, through having been broken in a fight during his first year in the police. Yet in Ingrid's

view he was a startlingly good-looking man. Not that she
had noticed this about him at first, or that many people
would have agreed with her. It was something that had
dawned on her little by little as she had come to notice
the way that his rather commonplace features could sof-
ten or light up with humour and sardonic intelligence. It
was, after all, a revealing face, although he did not intend
that it should be.

He arrived punctually at six that evening. Ingrid took
him into the small, square living room, which had a gas
fire in the black marble fireplace, an elaborate plaster cor-
nice, overfilled bookshelves, a faded green carpet and a
number of aged, comfortable chairs. Settling him on the
sofa with a drink, she told him of Ruth's illness and he
said how sorry he was to hear of it and that he would go
up to have a chat with her presently, if she was feeling up
to it. When Ingrid told him that her mother had said that
he was not to do this on any account, because of the in-
fection, he replied that he never caught a cold.

Then he said, "You aren't looking on top of the world
yourself. You aren't coming down with it too, are you?"

She smiled and shook her head.

"What's the trouble, then?" He was always quick to be
anxious if he noticed any alteration in the way that she
usually looked, his power of observation often going some
distance ahead of his understanding.

"It's nothing," she said. "It's just that I've got problems."

"I've had problems all day," he said wearily, "trying to
sort out some of the mess some people make of their lives.
How they survive at all beyond infancy with the mental
equipment they've got is something to bewilder you.
Sometimes you feel the world's an almost infinitely toler-
ant place. You can live on into old age without ever hav-

ing done a single generous or intelligent action. That's how it looks to me anyhow on one of my blacker days."

"Is today a black day?" she asked sympathetically.

"Not specially," he said, "just sort of grey around the edges. Go on and tell me about those problems of yours. They'll make a change from the ones I'm used to."

"Not so very much of a change, I'm awfully afraid."

Pouring out a drink for herself, Ingrid sat down close to him and began to tell him the story of Lady Guest's dress, of Ronald Starkey's disappearance, of Lady Guest's absence from her home all day and of Sir Edward's odd behaviour in the afternoon.

It seemed to her that she talked for a long time without Martin interrupting her at all and she began to wish that he would insist on saying something, anything, on some quite other subject, so that the two of them could start to talk about themselves. She wished that he would reach out for her and hold her very tightly. But he only sat listening with the extreme attentiveness of which he was capable, and it was not until he was quite sure that she had nothing more to say that he contributed anything.

"So you think the old man murdered her," he said.

"Martin!" she exclaimed. "I never said . . ."

"You said everything else." He smiled at her kindly.

"But I didn't mean—well, suppose I did." She breathed out sharply. "But it isn't really possible, is it? Sending her dress to the Economy Centre afterwards, I mean—that makes real nonsense of the idea."

"People sometimes behave very strangely after committing murders," he observed as impersonally as if he were making a not very striking remark about the weather. "Particularly murders that happen when something comes unhinged all of a sudden in their brains and they kill without really having meant to. In that condition they can do extraordinarily mad things, every bit as mad as sending that dress to the Centre."

"Then you don't think it was just a practical joke?"

"Actually, that seems very much more probable, doesn't it?"

"What do you really think, Martin?"

"Nothing much at the moment. But d'you know what I'd do if I were you?"

"That's what I've been waiting for you to tell me."

"I'd go and talk to Mrs. Legge. Find out if she really collected those clothes from the Guest woman yesterday afternoon. And if she did, where did she put them and when did she put them into her car to take them to the Economy Centre, and where and when could the pink dress have been added to them. Because that seems to me one of the strangest parts of your story. How did that pink ball dress apparently walk in the night?"

CHAPTER 3

When Ingrid arrived at the Legges' bungalow the next
morning she found Stephanie Legge working in the garden. She was raking up the dead leaves that were scattered over the lawn and collecting them for a bonfire. She
was wearing her drooping jersey dress, an anorak, gardening clogs and a pair of plastic gloves. Her striking red
hair, which had probably started the day in a bun at the
back of her head, was hanging in loose strands about her
shoulders.

She had been working with a kind of ferocity before
Ingrid's arrival interrupted her, treating the leaves as if
they were opponents in some peculiarly difficult and demanding struggle. She did not stop raking for at least a
minute after Ingrid had opened the gate and come towards her.

At last, leaning on her rake, Stephanie remarked, "I
don't know why I do this. The Guests never sweep up
their leaves and every time we have a wind all the ones
from their garden get blown all over ours. But I can't bear
to see things untidy. I expect you've come to see Sandra.
She isn't up yet. That girl doesn't think the day begins till
midday. I don't know why. It's how she's been all her life.
I never could get her off to school in time. And Andrew's
playing golf. Would you like some coffee?"

It was not the warmest of invitations.

"No, thank you, and I'm sorry to drop in on you like

this," Ingrid answered, "but actually it was you I came to see. There's a bit of a problem about those clothes of Lady Guest's you brought in to the Economy Centre yesterday morning, and I thought the best thing would be to consult you about it."

"Why not consult Lady Guest?"

Stephanie looked as if she were impatient to start raking again.

"That's what I tried to do yesterday," Ingrid said, "but she wasn't in. And today it struck me that really you were the right person to ask."

"Well, come inside," Stephanie said, dropping her rake on the ground and starting to pull off her plastic gloves. "Though I don't see what problem there can be, apart from the state of mind of a woman who can throw out clothes like that. It isn't as if there's any real charity about it. There's no generosity in giving away things you don't value, no sense of sacrifice." She led the way to the house with hasty strides. "How's Ruth?"

"About the same."

"Lucky for her she's got you to look after her. If I'm ill it doesn't seem to occur to Sandra to do anything for me. And of course Andrew expects me to go on waiting on him as usual. It's my own fault, I know. I've spoilt them both. But sometimes one would like people to show a little appreciation of what one does for them."

Stephanie had gone to the back door of the bungalow. On the doorstep she kicked off her clogs and slid her feet into down-at-heel slippers. Shrugging off her anorak, she dropped it onto a kitchen chair.

"No sign of Sandra yet," she said. "That girl could sleep through an earthquake. Not that she really sleeps as late as this, she just lies and daydreams. I used to try to break her of the habit, but it was only hitting my head against a wall. I don't know where she gets it from. Andrew's never had the imagination for dreams, and I've never had the time. Well, come along."

Stephanie hustled Ingrid through the kitchen into the living room.

The shape of the room was almost exactly the same as that of the Guests, but in everything else it was as different as it could be. It had last been decorated at a time when it had been in fashion to have every wall covered with a different patterned wallpaper. One wall was a trelliswork of blue and white convolvulus, another was all white and gold Regency stripes, one was a plain pale blue, and the fourth was bright orange. They all had a faded look, almost as if they felt some discouragement because it was such a very long time since anyone had even noticed them. The curtains had the same flower pattern as the one wall. There were some odds and ends of indifferent reproduction furniture and a three-piece suite covered in very shiny blue acrylic velvet.

"Sit down and tell me what this is all about," Stephanie said. "If anyone's been complaining that I didn't bring the clothes in straightaway when Lady Guest gave them to me, let me tell you I'm busy enough as it is without doing odd jobs for her. There was no reason why she shouldn't have taken her things to the Economy Centre herself, but it would have been a bother and she knew muggins would do it if she was asked. But it happened that I wanted to work on fixing up Sandra's fancy dress for the evening—such a clever idea I'd had, using an old red dressing-gown of mine to make her into the Red Queen. And then, would you believe it, the wretched girl said she had a headache and that she wouldn't be seen dead in that dress and that fancy dress balls were something out of ancient history anyway and she wasn't going to go?

Well, I was so furious I haven't been speaking to her since, though I wore the costume myself, so my time wasn't entirely wasted. I'd been going to go as a witch, but the Red Queen was really much cleverer. But if anyone's been saying I ought to have found time to get into the shop in the afternoon—"

"No, no," Ingrid interrupted the flow, "it's nothing like that. We just wanted to be sure that you did pick up the clothes from Lady Guest in the afternoon before the ball."

"Well, I did. After four o'clock. Why? Has she been saying I didn't? I brought them into the shop in the morning, didn't I? If she's been complaining—"

"She hasn't," Ingrid said quickly. "It's just that the dress that she wore at the ball has somehow got in with the other things and we can't understand how it happened. I mean, if you collected them in the afternoon. She didn't add that dress to them this morning, did she?"

"No, she didn't. I haven't seen her."

"Did you notice the dress when you brought the bundle in to us?"

Stephanie seemed about to fire off one of her rapid answers, but changed her mind about it, holding back the retort behind tight lips. After a moment she said carefully, "Let me see if I've got this straight. That pink Edwardian dress Lady Guest wore at the ball was among the things I took to the Centre yesterday morning?"

Ingrid nodded.

"But that's impossible," Stephanie said. "Absolutely impossible. Look—I went over to the Guests on Friday afternoon, just about four o'clock, and Lady Guest handed out that collection of clothes. She didn't ask me in. She wouldn't. She's a most fearful snob and lets me see she doesn't think I'm good enough for her. Unless, of course, I can be useful, then she chases me down by telephone fast enough. Anyway, I took the clothes and I put them straight into my car, which was in the garage, and I locked the car. I remember distinctly I did. I didn't lock the garage, because of course we were going to take the other car out to go to the ball, but I know for certain I locked my car, leaving the clothes in it, ready to be delivered next morning. So how could that pink ball dress possibly have got mixed up with them?"

"It's certainly a puzzle," Ingrid said, "but it did get in with them somehow. I saw it there."

"Well, *I* didn't. Not that I looked at all carefully. But it sounds nonsense to me." Stephanie moved restively, as if Ingrid had already taken up enough of her time.

"Has anyone else got a key to your car?" Ingrid asked. "I mean, could anyone else have added the dress to the other things this morning?"

"Andrew and Sandra both have keys," Stephanie answered. "But what would they do a thing like that for? And how could they have got hold of the dress? Are you suggesting Andrew met Lady Guest yesterday morning before he went to the office—he doesn't always go in on a Saturday, but he did yesterday—and she gave him the dress and he added it to the things in the car?"

"Perhaps that's possible," Ingrid said. "Can you think of any other explanation?"

"But he'd never have done a thing like that without telling me," Stephanie said, sounding extremely positive. But as soon as she had spoken her face gave a sudden twitch, as if she found herself having to fight some unnerving emotion. "All the same, you can stay here and ask him yourself when he gets in from his golf if you don't believe me. It couldn't have been Sandra who did it, that's certain, because she didn't get up until after I'd driven off with the clothes. She's quite friendly with Lady Guest, of course. I don't know why, unless it's just that Lady Guest enjoys patronizing someone who looks at her with such starry-eyed admiration. I don't think it's at all good for Sandra. I've tried to teach her some civilized values, but that woman does her best to undermine everything I've done. You don't know how I regret the Guests having come here to live next to us. We used to have such nice neighbours, the Wades, the sort of people you could really count on to help you out anytime you needed it. I mean, if we went away they'd always keep an eye on the house for us, see the pipes didn't freeze and light the central heating up for us before we came home and all that sort of thing. But their daughter's married in Australia and they went out to join her and the Guests moved in. At first, you know, I thought they were going to be quite an acquisition to the neighbourhood and naturally I did my best to be friendly, but I'm afraid I'm not up to their standards." Stephanie gave a sarcastic little laugh. "She was only his secretary, you know, before they got married. But that's just the kind of person who makes the worst sort of snob. It's insecurity, I suppose. Perhaps I shouldn't be so critical. But she seems to unsettle everyone she comes into contact with. I'm sure her husband would be much easier to get along with if it weren't for her. After all, he takes part in all our local activities and seems quite anxious to sit on committees and do all the dull sort of work that has to be done."

"I wonder," Ingrid said, trying to think coherently in spite of Stephanie's flow of speech, "did you leave the car unlocked anywhere in the town yesterday morning before you came to the Economy Centre?"

"No, I'm sure I didn't. Why? Oh, I see, you think someone might have popped the dress into it while it was standing somewhere. That isn't very likely, is it? And actually I'm always very careful about locking the car when I'm in town, even if I'm only leaving it for a few minutes. But who'd do such an extraordinary thing at all, I mean, sending the dress to the Economy Centre?"

"Yes, that's what it always comes back to," Ingrid said. "Why do it at all?"

Stephanie put her head on one side, looking at her quizzically.

"There's something about all this that you haven't told me, isn't there, Ingrid? There's something worrying you that you haven't said anything about."

Ingrid hesitated. But Stephanie was certain to obtain all the facts about the dress, perhaps with some gruesome embellishments, from one of the other women who had been in the Economy Centre yesterday morning, so what was to be gained by keeping them back now?

"It's just that there are some stains on the back of the bodice," Ingrid said, "which look awfully like bloodstains, and there's a hole in it that we—I mean Mrs. Belcher and the rest of us who were there yesterday—we thought it just could be a bullet hole. And we'd have gone to the police about it except that there was something so lunatic about sending the dress to the Centre that we thought it might turn out to have been a practical joke. So I talked it over with Martin yesterday evening and he advised me to find out from you just when you collected the other things from Lady Guest and when the ball dress could have been added to them."

"I see." Stephanie's gaze on Ingrid's face hardened, then she turned her eyes away to the big picture window, which, like the Guests', showed only the smooth green of the golf course beyond the low wall that bordered the garden at the back of the house and the darker green of the distant pines. After a while she gave a slow sigh.

"I should think you're right, it's that woman's idea of a joke," she said. "Perhaps she got Sandra to unlock the car for her in the night and put the dress into it then. Don't ask me to explain the mind of a person who thinks it's worth doing a thing like that, but it's really the only explanation, isn't it? I'll ask Sandra about it when she comes down, then I'll ring you up to tell you what she says. Of course, she'll lie about it, but I can generally get the truth out of her in the end. Anyway, I'll do my best."

Ingrid got up to go. But just then the gate in the low garden wall that led straight out on the golf course was opened and Andrew Legge came striding across the strip of lawn between the wall and the house, carrying a bag of golf clubs. In a moment he had disappeared round a corner of the house.

Stephanie laid a hand on Ingrid's shoulder, pressing her back into her chair.

"Wait a minute," she said. "I'll tell Andrew about all this and we'll see what he has to say. It may be interesting."

There was an odd glint in her eyes as if for some reason she felt pleasure in the thought of telling the story of the dress to her husband. Almost a spiteful pleasure. It made Ingrid feel embarrassed, as the emotions of her elders often did. But she sank back into her chair and waited.

After a moment Andrew Legge came into the room.

He was about the same age as Stephanie, a tall man, well-built except for a slight paunch, and he would have been handsome if his head had not been so small. Perched on his wide shoulders and thick neck, it looked almost as if it had been designed to fit another person.

But all in a small-scale way, his features were finely modelled, with a rosy mouth, healthily pink cheeks, a short straight nose, amiable grey eyes and straw-coloured hair, which he wore rather long, curling up a little above his heavy blue turtleneck sweater.

"Well, well," he said, seeing Ingrid and giving her a welcoming smile which showed small, gleaming teeth. "Our lovely gypsy without her disguise, but just as lovely as ever."

"Your gypsy has a very strange story to tell you," Stephanie said. "Go on, Ingrid, tell him what you've just told me."

Ingrid was beginning to feel more than a little tired of telling the story. But this need not have bothered her now, for she had hardly begun it when Stephanie interrupted, taking it over from her and speaking very fast and with an increasing relish that Ingrid found difficult to understand. Was it simply that Stephanie enjoyed the little mystery, she wondered, or could it be that she was actually titillated by the thought that Leila Guest might have been shot and killed wearing the beautiful dress?

As Stephanie went on, a note almost of accusation came into her voice and she kept her eyes, still with a brilliant glint in them, steadily on her husband's face.

It became puzzled to begin with, then flushed a dull red.

"Well, well," he muttered. It was an expression that he was very fond of. It filled in a little time without committing him to anything. "Well, well."

"Well, well," his wife echoed him mockingly. "And what do you think about it, Andrew?"

"I don't know. I haven't the least idea. I can't make any sense of it." He sounded angry in a subdued kind of way.

"Then I'll tell you something you can do," Stephanie

said. "You can ring up the Guests and ask them over for drinks."

He looked startled. "What, now?"

"Yes, now. It's nearly time for drinks, isn't it?"

"I don't understand. Why d'you want me to do that?"

"To find out if Lady Guest is around or if she's—vanished."

"What nonsense!" he exclaimed. "No, I won't do it. *You* do it, if you want to, but I'm not going to have anything to do with it."

"Could that be because you know something about what's happened to her?"

"You're mad. I haven't seen her since the ball." He crossed to a tray of drinks on a table against a wall and stood contemplating it gravely, as if it presented some serious problem to him. "Ingrid," he said after a moment, "sherry, gin?"

"No, thank you," Ingrid said, standing up. "I must be getting home."

Stephanie ignored her. Her eyes remained on the back of her husband's small head with the brightness that had that disturbing look of satisfaction in it.

"Go on, ring them up, ask them over, see what happens," she said.

"Nothing will happen," he answered. "You couldn't expect them to come at such short notice."

"Why not? Good neighbours would. Good friends, I mean, who aren't intolerable snobs. And specially if you ask them to come. You always defend them if I criticise them. You get on so well with them. So go on and ask them over."

"I won't," he said again. He poured out a stiff whisky for himself, then drank half of it down, standing where he was with his back to the room.

"*I'll* do it, then." Stephanie sprang to her feet and made an almost catlike pounce on the telephone and began dialling rapidly.

Ingrid wondered at her knowing the number by heart if she was really on as bad terms with the Guests as she made out, then she remembered that the people who had lived in the bungalow before them had been close friends of the Legges' and that the number of the telephone had probably not been changed.

"Oh, Sir Edward?" Stephanie said. "This is Stephanie Legge . . . Yes, the ball was a great success, wasn't it? I hope it actually made a profit. I always feel there's something rather indecent about capering about for one's own enjoyment and pretending one's really doing it to help the starving and the helpless. But that isn't what I rang up to say. Andrew and I just wondered if you and Lady Guest would come over for drinks . . . Oh? . . . Oh, is she? I see . . . Well, I'm sorry, but perhaps some other time . . . Yes, of course." She put the telephone down. "There!" she said. "Isn't that interesting?"

"Since we don't know what you were told . . ."

Andrew strolled across the room and planted himself on the hearth rug.

"Leila, dear Leila," Stephanie said, attempting a mocking imitation of Edward Guest's voice, "is away on a visit to some friends. She went away yesterday and he doesn't know when she's coming back. She hasn't decided. But they'll be *so* glad to come over for drinks when she returns. Isn't that nice of them? And isn't it *very* interesting?"

Andrew's neat little features showed a fleeting surprise, then settled into an expression of irritation. "She didn't say anything to me on Friday evening . . . Anyway, what's so extraordinarily interesting about it? Doesn't she quite often go away to stay with friends? She seems to have plenty of time."

"But it hasn't ever happened the day after the dress she wore the evening before has turned up with bloodstains and a bullet hole, has it?"

"You're talking poisonous rubbish," he said. "Dangerous, at that. I believe it's a libel to say a person's dead if they aren't."

"Have I said anyone's dead?"

"Isn't it what you mean?"

Stephanie gave a little laugh. "But you didn't know anything about her going away. You don't know a thing. And it worries you that you don't, doesn't it, dearest?"

Andrew raised a hand in a clenched fist. Like his head, his hands and feet were unusually small for a man of his size, yet for an instant that little fist looked threatening. Ingrid had a sense of something explosively violent in the room. Then he let the hand fall. He turned to Ingrid.

"Don't take any notice of Stephanie," he said. "She's always had too much imagination for her own good. I've told her she ought to write a book. Don't they say everyone's got at least one book in them? Sure you won't have a drink?"

"Yes, thank you, quite sure." This time Ingrid made her escape to the door.

But she had not yet reached the front door, with Andrew hurrying after her to open it for her, when she heard the flapping of sandals on the floor and saw Sandra Legge coming out of the kitchen, chewing a thick slice of bread and marmalade.

She was seventeen, a tall, clumsily built girl with the same small head and almost dainty features as her father, though compared with the firm, healthy pink of his complexion, hers looked doughy and colourless. Her hair was short and mousey. Her whole body was cushioned in a soft covering of fat, while her eyes had the lack of expression, almost the coldness, of someone who, as her mother had said, lives in dreams. Her response to other people was always unwilling and lethargic. She was wearing stained blue jeans, a tight sweater that hugged her large breasts, and sandals with two-inch platform soles.

Ingrid paused in the open doorway. "Hallo, Sandra," she said.

Sandra mumbled something, chewing.

"Sandra!" her mother called from the living room. "So you got up at last. Come here. There's something I want to ask you."

"Yes, so there is," Ingrid said quickly, wanting a chance to get the question in herself. "Did you by any chance put a dress of Lady Guest's in with her other things in your mother's car sometime early yesterday morning—a pink Edwardian ball dress."

"Mm?" Sandra said questioningly through her bread and butter.

"Someone did, you see."

"Funny."

Andrew put an arm round Sandra and patted her plump shoulder.

"Sandra doesn't know anything about it, do you, love?" he said.

She leant confidingly against him, shaking her head. But the curious thing was that for an instant Ingrid had seen fear on the girl's face. She was sure that it had been fear. Not that it was easy to interpret the very faint changes of expression which were the most of which those dull features seemed to be capable. Ingrid wished that Andrew would go away and leave the girl to her for a few minutes, but he remained where he was, his arm still round his daughter.

Ingrid said goodbye and went towards the gate. Before she reached it Stephanie came running after her.

"Ingrid, Ingrid, wait!" she panted. "I did leave the car unlocked for a few minutes in town. I'd parked just in front of the Co-op and gone in to do a little shopping. I remember I was annoyed with myself when I got back to the car and found what I'd done for once. But I don't suppose it's important. Well, goodbye."

"Goodbye," Ingrid said again and went on to the Mini.

When she reached home she found Ruth in bed with a temperature still of a hundred and one. But she remained adamant that the doctor should not be called.

"This sort of thing just has to run its course," she said. "There's no point in making a fuss about it."

"What would you like for lunch?" Ingrid asked.

"Nothing much. An egg. Or some soup. Whatever's the least bother. You know, Ingrid, I've been thinking."

"What about, in particular?"

"About everything. Ronald. He still hasn't telephoned or anything. And the dress. Well, I've come to the conclusion that the only possible explanation of it all is that it's a practical joke and Ronald's at the bottom of it. You know what he's like, he's got a very odd sense of humour."

"Yes, that's true, but how did he get hold of the dress? How could anyone have got hold of it but one of the Guests?"

"Oh, I haven't thought out the details," Ruth said. "But suppose Ronald went home with them for a drink after the ball and Leila got out of the dress straightaway because it was killing her, and he got hold of it somehow and took it away with him and then thought it would be funny to make it look as if murder had been done, just to frighten us at the Economy Centre? I'm afraid he's capable of it."

"I'm sure he is," Ingrid said, "but I still don't see how he could have got the dress into Mrs. Legge's car unless one of the Legges was in the joke with him, and that doesn't seem likely, does it? Mrs. Legge says she picked up the other clothes from Lady Guest on Friday afternoon and left them in her locked car overnight. The only possibility is that Ronald somehow managed to pop the dress into the car when it was standing in front of the Co-op yesterday morning. Mrs. Legge told me she left it there unlocked for a short time while she did some shopping. But d'you know, I've been wondering . . ." She paused, plucking at the eiderdown on the bed. "Perhaps it's a fantastic question, but d'you think there's ever been anything between Mr. Legge and Lady Guest?"

"Oh, my goodness!" Ruth exclaimed. She gave a whoop of laughter which degenerated into a fit of coughing. She wiped her watering eyes. "What made you think of that?"

"Only that Mrs. Legge obviously thinks there has been," Ingrid said.

"Oh, Stephanie! If she saw Andrew give a drink to some woman at a party, she'd think there was something between them. You know, it's very sad. I remember when she first came to live here, she was a really quite beautiful woman. She'd that gorgeous hair and a figure I used to envy immensely and she even dressed quite reasonably too. And then something seemed to go wrong with her. I don't know what it was. I suppose she and Andrew have never been really right for one another. Look at the mess they've made of that daughter of theirs. But I can't imagine Andrew getting very far with Leila, though perhaps if she was really bored . . ." She stopped, as if she felt that she had been talking too freely. "If Ronald or anyone else put the dress in the car when it was outside the Co-op, someone's sure to have seen it, don't you think?"

"I suppose so," Ingrid agreed.

"And tracking down witnesses—I mean, if something's happened to Leila—is a job for the police, isn't it? So perhaps if you spoke to Martin . . ."

"Yes, perhaps I'll try that. Now about lunch, you'd like an egg?"

"I think I'd really like just some soup and a piece of toast," Ruth said, "if that would be quite easy."

Ingrid went downstairs, opened a tin of Scotch broth and heated it up. She herself ate some bread and cheese. Presently she made coffee. Ruth took two aspirins with her coffee, then seemed inclined to settle down to sleep. Ingrid took her tray downstairs and washed up the things that had been used. She was just putting them away in the china cupboard when the telephone rang. She went to answer it.

"Ingrid?" a woman's voice said. "It's Edith Laker. How's Ruth? Can I speak to her?"

"Well, she's in bed and I think she's asleep," Ingrid answered, "and I'd sooner not disturb her."

"No, no, of course not," Edith Laker said. "It's just that I'm very worried. But it can wait."

"Shall I give her a message when she wakes up?" Ingrid asked.

"Oh, it doesn't matter. Oh well, perhaps you might. You see, I was expecting the Guests for lunch today and they never came. Never telephoned or anything. And that's so unlike them. Lady Guest might be forgetful, but Sir Edward's so punctilious. So I began to wonder if we'd somehow muddled up the date and I telephoned them and Sir Edward answered and he seemed to have forgotten all about the lunch and he said his wife had gone away on a visit to some friends and he sounded—oh dear, Ingrid, I'm sure I shouldn't be saying this, but honestly he sounded drunk. So, as Ruth knows them much better than I do, I thought I'd ask her what she thinks and whether it seems to her one ought to do anything. Because . . ." Edith's voice faltered. She fell silent.

Because, Ingrid finished the sentence for her in her own mind, we found a bloodstained dress with a bullet hole in it, and the best of husbands have been known to kill their wives and announce that they have gone away to stay with friends.

And that's two people suddenly missing, she added to herself. Does that sort of thing happen by chance?

"Of course, the last thing one wants to do is to interfere," Edith Laker went on. "I mean, in what almost certainly isn't one's business. All the same . . ." Again her voice faded.

"Of course," Ingrid agreed. "Well, I'll tell my mother about it when she wakes up, shall I?"

"Yes, please do. Thank you. And ask her to phone me when she feels well enough and tell me what she thinks."

Edith rang off.

Ingrid put the telephone down. But her hand stayed upon it as she stood there, looking thoughtfully before her. An uncertain frown appeared on her face. She began to pluck at her lower lip. Then abruptly, her mind suddenly made up, she started to dial the number of the police station in the castle. Martin had told her not to make private calls to him there, but this was not exactly a private call.

The voice that answered her told her that Inspector Rhymer was engaged and asked if someone else could help her. She said that it had to be Inspector Rhymer or no one. She was asked to wait. The wait was a long one, but at last she heard Martin's voice.

"Inspector Rhymer speaking."

She began, "It's Ingrid—" But before she could say any more he broke in, "Oh, for God's sake, not now. I'm in the middle of something. What is it? I'll call you back later."

"But, Martin, this is important—"

"I'll call you later."

"No, wait, please wait just a minute. It really is important. It's about that dress."

"What dress?"

"That pink Edwardian ball dress I told you all about yesterday."

"Oh yes, that. Well?" He sounded tense with impatience.

"Well, I went to see the Legges this morning, as you said I should, and Mrs. Legge said she picked up the other clothes from Lady Guest in the afternoon before the ball and put them in her car and that the car was locked, so no one could have put the dress into the car after that except her husband or daughter, except for a few minutes when the car was outside the Co-op on Saturday morning, and—"

"Ingrid, I really haven't got time to listen to all these details," Martin interrupted her, obviously having to make an effort to make his voice sound pleasant. "Go straight to the point. What are you trying to tell me?"

She let her voice rise. "That Lady Guest's missing! No one's seen her since Friday night. And her husband's told Mrs. Legge and Miss Laker that she's gone away to stay with friends, when he told me yesterday she was just out somewhere and he seemed to be expecting her back soon. And Miss Laker said he sounded drunk when she telephoned and I think there was something between Lady

Guest and Mr. Legge and Mrs. Legge knows it, and Ronald Starkey's still missing, and—"

"And so one of them murdered the woman, that's what you're leading up to," Martin interrupted again. "Shot her in the back, but his heart bled so for the starving millions of Bangladesh that he stripped her and donated her dress to charity. Look, I really haven't got time to talk about this now, Ingrid, but I'll ring you later."

"I shouldn't bother." Ingrid carefully lowered her voice. She did not quite intend it, but it suddenly turned icy. "Of course, when you put it like that I can see I'm being absurd and I'm sorry I troubled you."

"Now, don't take it like that—"

"Just how do you want me to take it?"

"Only wait a little. Let me think it over."

"You don't really mean to think it over, do you? You don't think it's important and you're too busy to bother. When I mentioned the dress, you'd forgotten all about it."

"Yes, I'm very sorry about that and I don't mean it isn't important."

"Don't you? I feel fairly sure it's just what you *do* mean. But it's all right. I'm sure everything will explain itself satisfactorily sooner or later. I may even be able to solve the puzzle by myself, and then I'm sure it'll turn out not to have been anything important at all. Goodbye."

"Oh, Ingrid, wait—"

But she did not wait. Yet when she had put the telephone down, her hand lingered on it again, as if something in her were protesting against her own cutting of the connection.

CHAPTER 4

At the other end of the line Martin, putting down the telephone, had the same feeling. He cursed himself for the way he had spoken to Ingrid. However, it was as he had said, he had no time just then to think about the pink dress that he had so tactlessly forgotten, or about Lady Guest. He was in the middle of an interrogation of a boy who had been brought into the police station the afternoon before on suspicion of shoplifting in one of the chain stores in the town. Martin knew there was no hope of holding the boy; nevertheless, the questioning had to continue. But it was certain that he would not be charged. By the time the store detective had managed to reach him through the Saturday afternoon crowd in the shop, the shirts to which he had seen the boy help himself from one of the open counters had been passed on into other hands. And he was not going to break down and tell the police anything about the other members of the gang with whom he had been working, a gang on whom they had been trying to lay their hands for some weeks. Martin had recognised almost at once that this boy was not of the kind that could be scared or cajoled into saying a word more than he thought judicious.

He was eighteen, a gangling youth with tangled hair to his shoulders, a wispy beard, thin, pallid cheeks and small, intelligent, evasive eyes. They were very hard eyes, as you could see on the rare occasions when he let them meet yours. Shoplifting, Martin was prepared to swear, would turn out to be only an early stage in a long career of crime.

It was nearly six o'clock when the boy was allowed to go home. But other work had piled up by then and Martin did not reach his lodgings until too late in the evening to telephone Ingrid. For even though she would certainly still be up, the ringing of the telephone might waken Ruth, which would be a pity.

That, at least, was the reason Martin gave himself for not telephoning as he had promised. That perhaps he simply did not want to speak to Ingrid just then was something he preferred not to think about. He had never been introspective. He had never had much success with analysing his own feelings and motives. He seemed to manage best if he ran his life according to a few fairly simple rules, and one of the very simplest of these was to avoid quarrels by telephone. It was altogether too easy to let them get out of hand. If there had to be a quarrel, then the only thing was to have it out face to face. That could be bad enough, but there was always the chance that if you could see each other, touch each other, the trouble would fade away into thin air.

Besides, this business of the pink dress that was so much on Ingrid's mind was much too complicated to sort out on the telephone. Dismissing it, Martin set out for a meal in the local Chinese restaurant, which luckily stayed open late.

All the same, at nine-thirty the next morning, when Clare Sykes arrived with the key to open up the Economy Centre, she found him in the doorway.

He introduced himself, and Clare's wan face lighted up.

"Oh, I'm so glad you've come," she said as she opened the door and led him into the shop. "I've been worrying and worrying. I said, the moment I saw the dress, 'That's blood and a bullet hole and we ought to call the police.' But the others all said I was hysterical. It isn't true, you know, I'm not in the least hysterical, it's just that I'm very sensitive about certain things, and blood's one of them. I simply can't bear the sight of it and I knew at once, from the way I felt about it when I saw it, that that was the only thing it could be. Would you like some coffee?"

"No, thank you," Martin said, "but if I could see the dress . . ."

"Yes, of course. We put it away very carefully. But I'll just put the kettle on first, if you don't mind. The others always like coffee when they get here."

She disappeared into the back room and Martin heard the sound of a kettle being filled.

After a moment she called out, "It's in here, if you don't mind coming through. The fact is—well, it gives me gooseflesh to touch it, so if you could just take it . . ."

He followed her into the back room. She had taken off her coat and was standing at the table, spooning instant coffee into mugs. The electric kettle had begun to sing.

She gave a rather furtive look towards a corner of the room.

"It's up there on the shelf," she said. "In that plastic bag. You'll want to take it away with you, I expect. I hope so. We've had some funny things brought in to us here— once we had a lot of lovely baby things that had all been got ready for a poor little baby that was born dead and I felt ever so sad and queer when I was selling them and I was really glad when they'd all gone—but there's never been anything as—as weird as that dress. Do please take it away. I feel kind of haunted while it's here."

Martin reached up to the shelf for the plastic bag through which he could see the sheen of pink satin.

"You'll want a receipt," he said.

"Oh, do you think that's necessary? I'm sure it isn't. I mean, as you're police and engaged to Ingrid and all, I'm sure it's quite all right for you to take it. I think Ingrid's a wonderful person, you know, I do really."

"All the same, I think it might be best if I gave you a receipt. I'll just take a look—"

"But not here—please not here!" Clare cried, putting her hands over her eyes.

"But perhaps if I can tell you it isn't blood and that there's no need for you to distress yourself—"

"It *is* blood, it is, I know it!"

"Don't watch, then," he said. "I'll open it up in the other room, and if there's the slightest chance you're right I'll take it away with me and have it tested. Now don't worry. There's no need for you to look on at anything if you don't want to."

Martin could sound very fatherly if he wanted to. Taking the plastic bag into the front room, he opened it and carefully extracted the folded ball dress.

After a longish silence, Clare called out, "Well?"

"I'll take it, Mrs. Sykes," Martin answered gravely. He began to refold the dress.

"It *is* blood, then!"

"At the moment I can only say it *may* be."

But really he had no doubts. He had seen enough blood in fights, in traffic accidents, and even once or twice in murder, to recognise it when he saw it. He had seen bullet holes less often, but if the hole in this dress had not been made by a bullet, he would never trust his judgement again.

"Now let me write that receipt," he said. "I'll let you know if we have to keep the dress."

He slid it back into the plastic bag, scrawled a receipt which he left for Clare on the counter and went out to his car.

In the car he sat for some moments with the bag on the seat beside him, considering the various things he might do next. What he at length decided to do was to telephone Ingrid to tell her that he had been a fool the day before not to have taken her more seriously. There was a call box at the corner of the street. He got out of the car again and went to it.

He heard the telephone ringing and ringing in the house and he was about to give up when he heard it lifted and Ruth say huskily, "Yes?"

"It's Martin," he said. "I'm sorry. I didn't mean to get you up. How are you?"

"At death's door," she answered. "You've just missed Ingrid. She's gone to the library to find me some thrillers to read. It's no use, I told her, I've read every thriller that ever was written. But perhaps she'll be lucky and find something I've forgotten. It's what's so splendid about thrillers, isn't it? You can read them over and over again and find you don't remember a single thing about them. Can I give her a message, Martin?"

"No. Yes. Perhaps. If you'd just tell her I've collected Lady Guest's dress from the Economy Centre and I'm going to have it examined."

"Oh good, I'm glad you're doing that," Ruth said. "She didn't think you'd bother."

"And I'll ring again later."

"Yes, do. I'll tell her."

They said goodbye to one another and Martin returned to his car.

But he did not at once take the plastic bag into the police station. Instead, he sat for a little while looking at the pink parcel beside him. He had folded the dress so that the hole and the stain did not show. It looked an innocent and charming piece of finery without a trace of anything sinister. But looking at it gave Martin a faintly

queasy sensation which he always felt more strongly than
he would ever have admitted to anyone when he encountered violence and death. He had a good deal more imagination than he gave himself credit for.

After a few minutes he started the car and drove off
down Castle Street away from the police station, taking
the turning halfway down the street that led towards the
golf course. The morning was grey and gusty. Dead
leaves were lifted from the pavements in swirls and a few
were driven fluttering like battered moths against his
windscreen. The tress that had been stripped of them
looked stark and wintry against the cloudy sky.

He had never been to the Guests' bungalow before, but
Ingrid had once pointed it out to him when they had
been driving past. He knew that the Guests had said a
number of times that he and Ingrid must come to dinner
sometime, but that was as far as the invitation had ever
got. Now he was glad of this. The interview ahead of him
was likely to be difficult enough without being complicated by past hospitality. Reaching the bungalow, he left
his car in the road, took out the dress in its plastic wrap-
ping and walked up the short drive to the door.

It was opened by a woman in an overall who was involved with the coils of a vacuum cleaner in the hall. She
said that Sir Edward was in and took Martin into the living room. Almost at once Edward Guest came hurrying
into the room, giving Martin the curious feeling that he
had been expected. He felt almost as if they had had
some appointment to meet and that he was late for it. But
a few steps inside the door Guest checked himself, then
advanced again more slowly, holding out his hand and
smiling.

"Inspector Rhymer? That's Ingrid Winter's Inspector
Rhymer, isn't it?" he said. "I've wanted so much to meet

you. Ruth Winter is one of my oldest friends, as I expect you know. Her husband and I were at school together. Poor Ruth was badly broken up when he died, but she's got tremendous courage and it's wonderful how she's managed to carry on, a great deal of it for Ingrid's sake, of course. My wife and I are immensely attached to her. We're very fond of Ingrid too. Now do sit down. What will you have to drink? Whisky, gin, beer?"

"Thank you, sir, it's a bit early in the day for me," Martin said.

He did not sit down. The two men faced each other across the hearth rug. Martin could feel impatience and expectancy in the other man, as if he already knew why Martin had come to see him. He was aware of forcefulness too in Guest and, in spite of the obvious tension in his trim, upright body, a habit of great self-control, of command over himself and no doubt of others. His eyes held Martin's and did not drop to the parcel that he was carrying.

"I came to ask you if you could identify this," Martin said, beginning to open the plastic bag. The satin folds spilled out.

He was certain that Edward Guest was startled. This was not what he had been expecting.

"My mother's dress!" he exclaimed. "The one my wife wore at the ball on Friday. You found it. How extraordinary. And how very kind of you to bring it back to me. I'm immensely grateful. I thought it was gone for good."

He smiled warmly.

"But I thought Ingrid came to see you yesterday to tell you how it had turned up at the Economy Centre, with some other clothes of Lady Guest's," Martin said.

"She did, she did," Guest said, "but it was such a strange story, I thought perhaps the dress had got confused with another one and somehow been put among my wife's clothes by mistake. Or something like that. I can't say I thought very clearly about the matter. I merely felt that what she told me was impossible."

"But you're certain this is the dress that belonged to your mother, are you, sir?" Martin asked.

"Oh, without the slightest doubt. That wonderful material—you couldn't get anything like it now for love or money. And there couldn't be two dresses just like that in this neighbourhood, could there? No, if you want a positive identification, I'm quite ready to give it."

But Guest's hands remained hanging at his sides. He did not reach out to take the dress.

Martin began gently to unfold it.

"Did Ingrid tell you about the stain and the hole?" he asked.

Guest started. "A stain? A hole?"

"Yes, I'm afraid so."

"No—no, I'm sure she didn't. I wonder if that explains . . . no, it couldn't. I hope the damage isn't serious. The dress happens to mean a good deal to me. Show me, will you?"

Martin turned the dress so that the stain on the bodice and the hole in it showed.

Edward Guest stood staring at it, and while he did so his lean, dark face went a shade paler. He pressed his lips together as if he were holding back words that came to his mind. At last he said quietly, "May I?" and reached out his hands.

Martin let him take the dress.

"It *is* blood, I suppose," Guest said.

"It looks like it, but it hasn't been tested by the pathologists yet," Martin answered.

"But you're going to do that, of course. Yes, you'd have to. So you won't be leaving it with me. No, naturally not." Guest thrust the dress back at Martin, almost as if he wanted it off his hands. "But you'll let me know the result, won't you? Tell me as much as you can about what happened."

"Then there's nothing you can tell me, sir?"

"No, I'm sorry."

"A moment ago you began to say that you wondered if the stain explained something, then you said it couldn't. Can you tell me what you meant by that?"

"I meant," Guest said, "that if my wife had somehow ruined the dress, she might have been afraid to admit it to me and might have had the fantastic idea of getting rid of it by sending it to the Economy Centre. But I dismissed the idea as soon as I thought of it. It's not in character for her to be unduly worried about a thing like that. And of course I didn't even know that the stain was probably blood."

"Didn't your wife give you any explanation of what had happened to the dress?"

"No."

"Didn't you notice that it was missing?"

"I didn't give it a thought. I—I had other things on my mind. I think perhaps . . ."

Guest turned towards a chair, dropped into it and lay back, crossing one knee over the other.

"I wish you'd sit down," he said rather irritably, as if the sight of Martin standing over him annoyed him.

Martin sat down facing him, the bright satin of the dress, with its frills of ivory chiffon, draping itself over his lap.

Guest brought the tips of his fingers together and

frowned at them doubtfully. His eyes were hidden by his drooping eyelids. He remained silent for some time. Martin waited patiently.

"I think perhaps," Guest went on, "I'd better do some talking. I'd hoped it wouldn't be necessary, at least not yet. But with the riddle of the dress and the problem of what may have happened to my wife on my mind, I realise I shall have to speak openly. You see, my wife has left me."

"I see," Martin said.

"I doubt if you do. I certainly don't myself. I thought we were a reasonably happily married couple. We had our troubles, of course, as you might expect with such a big difference of age between us. I'm sixty-one. She's only thirty-three. But I never thought there was anything seriously wrong."

"When did she leave you, sir?" Martin asked.

"On Friday, after the ball. Or rather, during the ball, though I didn't realise it at the time. She came to me about halfway through it and said she had a headache and wanted to go home. I was unwilling to leave myself. I'm on the committee of the League of Social Service whose show the ball was, and I felt I ought to see it through to the end. She said that was all right, she'd arranged with Mr. Starkey to drive her home. You may know Ronald Starkey. He's been lodging for the last few weeks with Mrs. Winter. He's my brother-in-law—that's to say, he's the brother of my first wife. I'm afraid he's rather my old man of the sea. He turns up out of the blue whenever it suits him and expects a helping hand. I've got rather tired of it, but for Caroline's sake I've done what I could for him. Anyway, he and Leila drove off together and I've never seen her since."

"Hasn't she been in touch with you? Hasn't she telephoned? Didn't she write you a letter?"

"She left a letter of a sort, yes. It was propped up on the mantelpiece there." Guest nodded at the fireplace between him and Martin. "It said that she was leaving me and that she'd get in touch with me when she'd decided what she was going to do. It gave no explanation of her action. It didn't give any address or telephone number where I could get in touch with her. And now I wish I'd kept it so that I could show it to you, but at the time I was so upset I simply crumpled it up and threw it into the fire."

"And you've heard nothing from her since?"

"Nothing at all."

"Do you know that Mr. Starkey hasn't been seen either since the evening of the ball?"

"Hasn't he?" Guest sounded indifferent. "Oh yes, I remember Ingrid said something about that. I told her not to worry."

"Then you don't think he and your wife may have left together?"

Guest raised his bushy eyebrows. "It would surprise me very much indeed if they had."

"He couldn't have been her reason for leaving you?"

"I think she actively disliked him. And I don't think the dislike she paraded was just a cover for being in love with him, if that's what comes to your mind. Naturally, I've considered it. But Leila's always found it very easy to dislike anyone who hasn't got money or who can't be useful to her in some way. If she's left me for another man, and that seems to me the most likely thing to have happened even if she didn't say so in her letter, then I think we'll find he's quite well-heeled, which Starkey isn't."

"What about Starkey's feelings for her?"

Guest gave Martin a hard stare.

"You're suggesting he shot her here out of jealousy because he found she intended to go off with some other man, and then he panicked and bolted, taking her body with him to hide it somewhere."

"I'm just exploring possibilities," Martin said.

"It *is* a possibility, I suppose. But she'd still have been wearing this dress, wouldn't she? Why should he have stripped her?"

"To make her body less easy to identify when it turned up again."

"But why—in God's name, *why* send the dress to that Economy place? It's as if he wanted to draw attention to the crime."

"And you don't think he would?"

"Would anyone?"

"It depends how unbalanced he was. There's an exhibitionist streak in a great many murderers."

Guest gave a short laugh. "Starkey isn't unbalanced at all. Twisted, yes, irresponsible, singularly childish. Well, perhaps that does mean he's unbalanced after a fashion. But if ever he committed a murder—and I don't think he really has it in him—he'd cover up his tracks very carefully. And apart from anything, I don't think Leila meant any more to Starkey than he did to her. If he had anything to do with the dress getting to the Economy Centre, then it was just one of his pranks. He'd a deplorable love of practical jokes. I can easily imagine him stealing the dress, which he might have been able to do if Leila changed out of it while he was still here, and somehow putting bloodstains on it, even if he had to cut his own finger to do it. Then perhaps he somehow persuaded Mrs. Legge to deliver the dress to the Centre with Leila's other

things. Have you considered that possibility? Mrs. Legge
has always had an intense dislike of Leila, and I don't
think she'd much use for me. She might have done what
Starkey wanted just to annoy us."

Martin looked down at the dark stain on the pink satin.

"It would have taken a pretty big cut on his finger to
make a stain this size," he said.

"Don't take me so literally," Guest said. "I spoke at ran-
dom. It may even not be human blood. Have you thought
of that? If the whole affair is some kind of nasty joke,
then that stain might have been made with, say, a juicy
piece of steak."

He seemed rather pleased with the suggestion and eyed
Martin with a little smile.

Martin stood up and began carefully folding the dress
so that he could put it back in the plastic bag.

Guest stood up too. The smile had quickly faded, leaving his handsome face expressionless.

"I'm sorry, I'm afraid you think I'm flippant," he said
gravely. "And perhaps cold-hearted. You'd be wrong on
both counts. I'm simply bewildered. In a state of shock. I
don't know how one's supposed to behave when one's
wife leaves one, but what I've been doing is drinking too
much and telling everyone lies. Lies everyone's beginning
to see through, I imagine. But I've kept hoping, quite un-
realistically, that if I say nothing Leila will suddenly
reappear. Just walk in anytime and we'll be able to pretend none of this trouble happened. I know she won't, of
course. I don't really deceive myself. She'd been behaving
oddly for some time before Friday night, and if I'd had
any sense the thing wouldn't have come as the surprise it
did. But I preferred not to notice the signs."

"The signs, sir?" Martin said.

"Yes, that for some reason she was very unhappy. I

don't much care to talk about it, but for one thing she'd suddenly taken to drinking by herself. Drinking quite heavily. And what does that mean but unhappiness? Perhaps she was simply desperate to get away because she couldn't stand our life here any more. Perhaps there isn't any other man. I'm honestly not sure."

"Do you know what her blood group is?" Martin asked.

Guest gave another small smile. "You stick to the point, don't you, Martin? No, I'm afraid I don't. But she went to the infirmary for a general checkup soon after we got here. She'd been run down and they gave her the works—blood pressure, electrocardiogram, blood samples, a barium meal, everything. Perhaps they've kept a record of it."

"Thank you."

Edward Guest saw Martin to the door, shook hands with him again and as he walked away to his car, stood in the doorway, watching him thoughtfully.

Back at the police station, Martin took the dress to the police laboratory and asked them there to check up on the nature of the stain. He warned them that the blood, if it turned out to be blood, might not be human, since there was a possibility that a gruesome joke had been played on the ladies of the Economy Centre. After that he made another telephone call to Ingrid.

She was in this time and as soon as she heard his voice said, "Oh, Martin, Mother told me you'd picked up the dress this morning. I'm so grateful. I thought you hadn't taken me seriously."

She sounded eager and anxious, as if the quarrel that they had nearly had on the telephone the day before had been distressingly on her mind ever since.

"I wanted to tell you," he said, "it's with the lab people

at the moment and it won't take them long to find out if the stain's blood and they'll probably be able to tell if the hole was made by a bullet. If the answer's yes, I'll take the affair higher. Satisfied?"

"Yes, oh yes."

"Incidentally," he went on, "I went to see your friend Guest this morning. I was Inspector when I arrived, but Martin by the time I left. Is that significant? Anyway, he identified the dress positively as the one his wife wore at the ball. Ingrid, what about meeting me for a drink this evening? Can you leave your mother?"

"Yes, once I've got her supper," Ingrid answered. "She's got her radio and lots to read."

"About eight o'clock, then, in the Anchor."

The Anchor was one of their favourite meeting places. It was a quiet pub in a narrow turning off Castle Street, not an interesting-looking building from the outside, but inside warm and comfortable and unpretentious. A flat-footed, placid, elderly woman, known as Mavis to the regulars, worked behind the bar.

Martin arrived before Ingrid and settled down at a corner table. A few minutes later Ingrid came in and, kissing Martin, said that she felt like a beer that evening and slid into the seat next to him. She had a sheaf of papers in one hand and when he had been to the bar and returned with a beer for each of them, she put the papers down before him.

"Look," she said, "I went to Fordham and Knowle's this afternoon and I got these." Fordham and Knowle's were the biggest house agents in the town. "They kept trying to put me off with ridiculous things—huge mansions miles out of town, or slums in the worst part of Pottershill. Honestly, don't you think house agents are mental? But I weeded these few out and, if you like, I'll go round to them tomorrow. I suppose you haven't got time to come with me?"

"I'm sorry, not tomorrow," he said. "And don't waste your time plodding round these places unless there's really some hope they'll be what you want."

"Well, take a look at them." She thrust the papers towards him. "See if there's one you like the sound of."

"I'll leave it to you," he said. "You're much better at that sort of thing than I am. Ingrid, about the stain on that dress . . ."

"Yes?"

"It's blood all right. Group O. That happens to be Lady Guest's blood group. They'd a record of that at the infirmary. But it's also the commonest group there is."

Ingrid gathered up the papers that she had put down in front of Martin and put them into her handbag. A brightness that had been on her face when she came in left it. Its sombreness gave it a sudden, rather alarming look of maturity.

"So it's murder," she said.

"Well, the hole in the dress was almost certainly made by a bullet, fired at fairly close range. I've put the facts before Nickerson and he thinks there's enough evidence to start an official inquiry."

Detective Superintendent Nickerson was Martin's superior officer.

"Oh God," Ingrid said in a low voice, "now that we've set things going, it feels awful. It seems an awful responsibility all of a sudden, almost as if it would have been better to say nothing about it. What will they actually do?"

"First try to trace Lady Guest. She wasn't out at the bungalow this morning, of course, and Guest's changed

his story about her again. He's given up saying she's gone
to stay with friends and says she's left him. Says she left a
note for him on Friday evening, telling him she was
going, but not where or with whom, and he felt so upset
he threw it straight into the fire. He says she left the ball
early with Starkey, but doesn't think she went away with
him because she didn't even like him. His suggestion
about how the dress got to the Centre is that it was a joke
of Starkey's."

"That's what Mother thinks."

"And he thinks Starkey may have been aided and abet-
ted by Mrs. Legge. What do you think about that?"

Ingrid looked puzzled. "How could she have helped
him?"

"Well, if he gave her the dress and she added it to
Lady Guest's other things out of malice. In a way, it's the
simplest explanation of how it could have happened."

Ingrid gave her head a decisive shake. "It's impossible.
I know Mrs. Legge doesn't like the Guests, but I'm sure
she'd never do anything as mean as that. She's a very puritanical sort of person with fearfully high standards of
morality. She'd never play tricks on anybody."

"Don't quite a lot of puritanical people go in for having
a very crude sense of humour?" Martin said.

"My guess is she's got no sense of humour at all."

"Then, we're not much further. Ingrid, you know Guest
fairly well, don't you?"

"Not really. Mother does. Why?"

"He gave me a rather odd piece of information. He said
his wife had taken to secret drinking."

"Secret drinking—Lady Guest!" Ingrid shook her head
again so positively that her dark hair swung about her
face. "She drinks quite a lot quite openly at parties and
things. But secretly—I don't believe it."

"But why should he have said anything about it if it wasn't true? He was talking pretty freely, as people in a state of great tension sometimes do and later wish they hadn't, but why should he make up a thing like that?"

"Why is it important, anyway?"

"I don't know. Perhaps it isn't. But anything can be important."

She frowned thoughtfully. "He puzzled me yesterday, you know. He's generally so reserved, but he talked quite a lot, much more than he usually does. I felt sure he was upset about something. Of course I didn't know anything then about his wife having left him."

"Or his having murdered her."

She met his eyes steadily, then, with a little shiver, dropped her head onto her hands. "I wish, I do wish that I'd never started this. Is that how you ever feel, Martin, when an investigation gets going? Do you ever feel there's something awful about smashing your way into people's private lives, perhaps perfectly innocent people, and stirring up you don't know what?"

"Yes, as a matter of fact, I do," Martin answered. "Sometimes even when they aren't all that innocent. Innocence and guilt have a way of overlapping, and sometimes you find your sympathies have gone to the wrong people and you can't even say why. And that's when you've got to be extra careful. It's when you're trying to fight your own feelings that you're most likely to let some pointless brutality in yourself get out of hand."

She gave him a look of surprise. "I shouldn't have thought you'd ever feel like that. I thought you were someone who had a way of always seeing your duty very clearly and controlling yourself very effectively."

"Don't ever think that about me." But he was rather surprised himself at what he had said. He was not even

sure that he meant it. And he was even more surprised to
find that Ingrid should have such an idea about him. It
scared him a little. She often scared him for reasons that
he could not quite understand, particularly when he was
feeling tenderest towards her. "Mind you, it doesn't have
to be Guest who murdered the woman. There's even some
evidence against it."

"Really and truly against it? I do hope you mean that."

"Well, she's supposed to have gone home halfway
through the ball because she had a headache, and
whether it was because she really had a headache or because she was going to meet some man who'd come to
fetch her, it's hardly likely she'd have stayed around,
wearing that Edwardian dress, until Guest got home. And
that, according to Guest, wasn't until after the ball ended.
So if she was shot while she was wearing the dress, it
looks as if it must have been before Guest got home."

"Did Ronald do it?"

"Now you're jumping to conclusions."

"Isn't it a rather obvious conclusion? I mean, the two of
them vanishing at the same time. He killed her, then
panicked and went into hiding."

"It could be pure coincidence. It's a great pity for a
poor policeman that coincidences keep on happening all
the time. And what motive had Starkey for killing Lady
Guest?"

"You'd never be able to guess with Ronald. It might be
something quite fantastic. Perhaps something from the
past. Something to do with his sister. It's a fact that he's
vanished, anyway, as if he's afraid to stay around."

"You may be right." Martin picked up one of her hands
and began absently playing with her slim fingers. "But
first we've got to check that Lady Guest really did leave
the ball with Starkey halfway through it and that Guest

stayed till the end. We'll have to find witnesses. So far there's only his statement that that's what happened. Ingrid . . ."

"Yes?"

"D'you think I'm wrong to want a home to go to straightaway when we marry?"

She did not answer at once, then she spoke slowly. "Sometimes I do. But I know it means a great deal to you because of what went wrong the first time, so we'll find one somehow, even if we have to lower our standards."

"It isn't only what went wrong before," Martin said. "If you saw what I do almost every day in my job, the squalor, the crazy instability and the ugliness, you'd want to make your own life as unlike it as you could."

"But one's home isn't everything. The Guests have a nice home, haven't they? Yet they don't seem to have been exactly happy."

"No, but . . . Well, never mind. Let me take another look at those particulars you got from Fordham and Knowle's. Perhaps, as you said, we could lower our standards."

For the next hour they did not talk about murder.

It was about half past ten when they drove home. There were a good many people about in the streets, mostly the young, and several groups of them were rowdily drunk. Martin saw two constables dealing with a knot of them. But, happily, they were no concern of his that evening, and anyway, the constables appeared to be on top of the situation. It was as his headlights swept past the doorway of a small dairy on a corner, where a couple stood embraced, that his mind became suddenly alert. He recognised that tangled hair, that gangling form. Not that it was important at the moment, but it was automatic for him to take notice of it.

He was startled when Ingrid exclaimed, "Martin, that was Sandra!"

"Sandra?" he said vaguely.

"The Legges' daughter. In that doorway. Didn't you see her?"

"I was looking at the boy," he answered.

"I wonder if her parents know she's out," Ingrid said. "I bet they don't. They've done everything they could to keep her a child. She's so dim, though, I didn't think she had it in her to pick up a boyfriend."

"Well, it's a pity she's picked up the one she has," Martin said, "because he happens to be the reason I was too busy to talk to you yesterday. He's in with a gang of shoplifters and he'd been brought in for questioning. Not that we've been able to make any charge stick yet, though I had a good try at it. But we're bound to get him sooner or later. So if you've any friendly feelings toward Sandra, Ingrid, even if she's dim, I think you might warn her."

CHAPTER 5

They took some time to say goodbye to one another at Ruth's door, then Ingrid slid her key into the lock as quietly as she could and gently pushed the door open, hoping not to waken Ruth. But her voice immediately called out, "Ingrid? Martin?"

He had been about to turn away, but hearing Ruth's call, he followed Ingrid inside.

The light in the hall was on and Ruth came out of the living room, clutching her dressing-gown round her.

"What are you doing out of bed?" Ingrid asked. "You promised to stay there."

"Yes, but I started thinking," Ruth replied. Her voice was thick and hoarse. "There's something about having a temperature that seems to make my brain abnormally active. And almost as soon as you'd gone out I had this idea, and after a bit I thought I might just as well do something about it as lie there worrying and doing nothing. And I've discovered something perfectly extraordinary."

She thrust out towards Ingrid a sheet of paper that she was holding.

"Well, let's go into the living room," Ingrid said as she took it. "It's horribly cold out here. I'm sure you oughtn't to have got up."

"That doesn't matter," Ruth said impatiently. She mopped at her nose. "I'm glad Martin's here. He can tell us what he thinks we ought to do. Actually, I'm feeling

rather guilty about what I did, but I thought that somebody had to do something." She followed Ingrid into the
living room, sat down close to the gas fire and put her feet
on the fender. "You see, I thought that if I hunted about
in Ronald's room, I might find the address of that sister of
his, Barbara. You know he had two sisters, Caroline and
Barbara, and Caroline's dead, of course, but I remembered he once said something about Barbara having married a farmer and living in Hertfordshire. I don't think he
ever saw much of her. Caroline was the one he was fond
of. All the same, I thought if I could find Barbara's address and telephone number, she might have some idea
about where he was likely to have gone. So I hunted
through that little desk in his room and I found an address book with her address and number in it, and I was
going to try calling her when I—I caught sight of that."
She nodded at the sheet of paper that she had given to
Ingrid. "And I recognised the handwriting. It's Caroline's.
I knew it because I used to get Christmas cards and an
occasional letter from her. But the odd thing that struck
me about this letter was that it was in a plastic envelope.
And at first I thought that was very touching, because it
must mean Ronald really treasured perhaps the last letter
he ever had from her. But then I—well, I read it, and . . .
Do please read it, Ingrid, and show it to Martin, and tell
me what you think about it, because I'm afraid it isn't
touching at all."

Ingrid started to read the letter, holding it so that Martin could read it over her shoulder.

It was written in a tight, nervous little scrawl, with no
address at the top, and the only date on it was July 17th,
without any year. But the paper, which was thin, of the
kind commonly used for airmail, was yellowish, as if the
letter were of a fair age.

It began:—

Dearest Ronnie,

There's a possibility that I'm going mad, but please take seriously what I'm going to tell you. I've got to tell someone, I can't keep it bottled up any longer. I believe Edward is trying to kill me. I know he wants to get rid of me, I've known that for some time, because he's fallen in love with that new secretary of his, Leila Dereham. She's very beautiful, much more so than I ever was, even when I was young, and she's young too, and he's the age when it happens to men, so I've been told. But why should he want to kill me, with poison too, so cruel and treacherous? If he really wants to get rid of me, why doesn't he simply tell me? I'd go home without making a fuss. Of course there'd be a bit of scandal, but that really doesn't matter much nowadays, does it? And he's so near to retirement anyway that he wouldn't lose anything to speak of, even if he had to give up his job. Of course, he'd hate being talked about, he's always been like that, but wouldn't it be better than doing something so frightful to me? We used to be very happy once, wonderfully happy. Doesn't that mean anything? I don't know what he's using, but I get the most terrible attacks of pain and vomiting, and when they happen to me, Edward just sits and looks at me, as if he's waiting, waiting. Ronnie, I don't know what to do. He makes out he wants me to see a doctor, but I'm sure if I agree I'll get the last big dose that'll finish me off before I see the man, and then Edward will persuade everyone it's suicide or something. No one would ever suspect him of murder, would they? I know they all say I'm hysterical and unstable and that Edward's wonderful to put up with me so patiently, but oh, if they only knew! Please, Ronnie, tell me what to do. Help me, help me soon!

Your loving

Caroline.

Towards the end of the letter the writing became even smaller than at the beginning and more of an illegible scrawl.

As she finished reading it, Ingrid let out a long breath.

"That can't be true, can it?" she said. "She died of cancer."

Martin reached over her shoulder, took the letter from her and started reading it again.

Ruth replied, "She died of barbiturate poisoning in Nairobi. They'd diagnosed cancer and she'd gone there for an operation. Edward went with her. I don't know what hope there was of her pulling through the operation, but I suppose if she'd done all right there'd have been another one soon and then another and she wouldn't have lived very long anyway. But in the hotel the evening before she was going into the hospital she took all the sleeping pills she'd been given, and Edward, who'd been out, came back and found her in a coma and she never came out of it."

"That's what Sir Edward himself told you, is it?" Martin said.

"Yes, and Leila too."

"Do you mean she was there?"

"Yes, I think she went along to help them on the journey. Caroline was very ill by then."

"But the pain and the vomiting that she wrote to Ronald about," Ingrid said, "that must have been the cancer, mustn't it?"

"I should think so." Ruth raised a sad face to look up at

Martin. "I don't believe a word of that letter, Martin. Edward always adored Caroline from the moment he met her. She was a wonderfully attractive woman, talented and amusing and at the same time very loving and gentle. So it looks to me . . ." She sighed. "Oh dear, I've always liked Ronald, as you know, partly because he sort of reminds me of Caroline, but I'm afraid it does look to me as if he may have come here to blackmail Edward with that letter. I mean, he kept it for some reason, didn't he? Kept it very carefully in that plastic envelope. And then there's the way he's stayed about here, doing nothing in particular, pretending he was writing—because I'm afraid you were right about that, Ingrid, he was just pretending. There isn't a trace of manuscript in his room. The only other papers in his desk were some unpaid bills. I'm sure, because once I started, I really searched. I felt awful about it, but at least, I thought, I was doing it for his own sake."

"What about his clothes?" Martin asked. "Did you check them? Are any of them missing?"

"I don't know," Ruth answered. "I've never counted his shirts and socks and I don't know how many suits he had, or suitcases even. He may have taken a case away with him. But that letter, I do assure you, there can't be a word of truth in it. Poor Caroline, I imagine she was out of her mind with pain and fear when she wrote it and probably wished next day she hadn't."

"You're absolutely sure there can't be any truth in it?"

A look of indignation appeared on Ruth's pale face.

"D'you realise you're saying Edward might have killed her?" she said. "For heaven's sake, it's absolutely unthinkable!"

"Well, Ingrid and I have been getting around to thinking that perhaps he murdered his second wife," he said, "so why not his first one?"

Ruth searched his face as if she were trying to make out if he was serious.

"You shouldn't talk like that, even when there's no one but Ingrid and me to hear you," she said. "I tell you, he and Caroline really did love each other. I know they did. Look at the way he's kept her piano, even though Leila longs to get rid of it."

"But for a time at least Caroline Guest thought that Guest was trying to kill her," Martin persisted.

Ruth gave a weary laugh. "D'you know, Ingrid, I believe Martin's interrogating me? It's the first time I've seen him behaving like a policeman. But I've told you, Martin, I'm sure Caroline was already very ill when she wrote that letter and was quite out of her mind."

"Is there any chance that she didn't write it?" Martin asked.

It took Ruth a moment to grasp his meaning, then she exclaimed, "You're thinking of forgery! You think Ronald could have forged that whole letter, then brought it here to blackmail Edward with. Can Ronald really be as awful as that? Have I been harbouring such a frightful criminal? And liking him too!"

"Lots of criminals are very likeable," Martin said. "I suppose you don't happen to have kept any old letters of Caroline Guest's."

"No, I don't think so. I don't go in much for keeping letters, once I've answered them."

"But perhaps Guest has something she wrote. If you don't mind my taking this letter with me, I can look into it."

"Is it all right to take it when really I stole it from Ronald's room?" Ruth asked. "Suppose he comes back and finds it's missing."

"I've a feeling that even if he does, he isn't going to make a fuss about it."

She considered the matter for a moment, then nodded. "All right, take it."

"Can I have the plastic envelope to keep it in?" he asked. "I don't want it damaged."

"I'll get it," Ingrid said and ran up the stairs to Ronald Starkey's room.

She saw the empty envelope lying on the small desk in front of the window. Beside it was the address book that Ruth had mentioned. Ingrid took them both downstairs. Martin carefully refolded the letter in its former creases and slipped it into the envelope. Seeing the address book, he said, "Do you mind if I take that too?"

"Wouldn't it be a good idea to try telephoning Barbara now?" Ruth suggested. "I know farmers go to bed early, but about something as important as her brother having gone missing for three days she wouldn't mind being woken up." She held out her hand for the little book and leafed through it. "Here we are—Barbara. He hasn't bothered to write down her surname and I don't remember what it is, but it's a Hertfordshire address, so I should think it's the right Barbara. Martin, will you try ringing her. My throat's so awful, I've hardly any voice."

He took the book, went to the telephone and dialled the number that Ruth had shown him.

The telephone rang for a long time before a man's voice at the other end asked gruffly, "What the hell?"

"I'm sorry to disturb you," Martin said, "but I'm ringing up for Mrs. Winter, Mr. Starkey's landlady. She's very concerned because he hasn't come home for three days."

"That little bastard," the voice replied. "Tell her she's well shot of him. Is that all you rang up about?"

"She thought perhaps you might have heard from him," Martin said.

"Christ, no. He knows better than to come round here after what happened last time. He came and settled on us for some weeks with some yarn about needing peace and quiet to finish some bloody book he was writing and he never even offered to contribute to the housekeeping. After a time I kicked him out."

"How long ago was that?"

"Oh, six weeks or thereabouts."

"Then, that was after he came back from New Zealand, was it?"

"New Zealand? He's never been near the place that I know of. I leave you to guess where he's really been. You shouldn't find it too difficult. Goodnight."

"Just a moment," Martin said. "Have you any idea where he might have gone when he left here?"

"To some woman, I should say. Sorry I can't tell you who. Goodnight."

Speaking quickly, before the connection could be cut, Martin said, "There's the problem of what Mrs. Winter should do about his belongings. His clothes are still in the room and his car's in the street."

"Give them to the Salvation Army, that's what I'd do. Is that all now?"

"Perhaps I should tell you Mrs. Winter has notified the police of his disappearance," Martin said.

"Aren't you the police yourself?" The sleepy voice was sardonic. "I'd say it's about time you got after him. It won't be the first time it's happened to him. Goodnight."

The telephone at the other end was put down.

Martin grinned as he put down Ruth's telephone. "I'm afraid your Ronald isn't those people's favourite relative," he said. "It was interesting, though, that the man said Starkey's never been to New Zealand. I think he was telling me he's really been in gaol. He tried living off his sister while he claimed to be writing a book, but his brother-in-law kicked him out. That was about six weeks ago."

"Oh dear," Ruth said, "so I've been dreadfully wrong about him, haven't I? It's very depressing. I do so hate being wrong about people."

"The only constructive suggestion that man on the phone made," Martin said, "was that Starkey was probably with some woman. I'll go through this book and see if I can find any lead to her. Now I'll leave you in peace. Go back to bed and please don't go on doing too much thinking. You've given me quite enough material to be going on with."

He stooped and kissed Ruth.

"Now you'll catch my cold," she said reprovingly. "And I've only been trying to help. I hope I have."

"If making things even more complicated than they were before is a help, then you certainly have." He put the plastic envelope and the address book into a pocket, took one more farewell of Ingrid in the hall and went out to the car.

Back in his lodgings, he went slowly through the address book. His lodgings consisted of one big room in a house in one of the few remaining Georgian terraces in Pottershill. It was an agreeable room with tall windows that opened on to small wrought-iron balconies, a high ceiling and a fireplace with an echo of Adam about it. But the only cooking facilities consisted of a small electric stove, a refrigerator and a diminutive sink in a cupboard that had once been a powder closet, and there was only one bathroom in the house, in which an average of a dozen lodgers came and went.

There was also the slight disadvantage of an all-too-friendly landlady, a woman to be avoided at all costs if it was important to arrive anywhere punctually. Once she had you cornered, she would not let you go. However, for about seven years Martin had been attached to the room for the sake of its fine proportions and an atmosphere of peace that it seemed to him it had. The furniture had come mostly from his old home in Gloucestershire, where his parents had been farmers. His elder brother had inherited the farm, but had brought his own furniture into the farmhouse and had allowed Martin to help himself to what he had wanted from among the not very distinguished antiques with which he had grown up. The result was comfortable and he liked it.

But he was determined that he and Ingrid were not to start their married life there. Not with that bathroom, not with that lack of a kitchen, not with kind Mrs. Bower fastening on to Ingrid every time she tried to go out shopping and holding her helpless in the strangling grip of her talk. Ingrid had repeatedly said that none of these things mattered, but he simply did not believe her. Hardly remembering his first marriage and yet deeply affected by it, he intensely wanted the stability of a home that should be very important to them both.

Sitting down by the electric fire that stood on his handsome hearth, he began to go through Ronald Starkey's address book. A good many of the entries were cryptic, mere initials with a telephone number. If Starkey did not reappear soon, some constable was going to have to spend some boring hours checking up on them all. Most of the numbers were in London. In Pottershill there were only two. One was the Guests', and the other belonged to someone designated simply by the letter J. J's telephone code number was the same as Martin's, which indicated that whoever it might be lived somewhere near him. He considered telephoning straightaway, but decided instead to try the number in the morning and went to bed.

He dialled the number at eight o'clock next day, hoping to catch J before he or she went out to work. He was answered at once by a light, girlish voice that said, "Oh, Ron!"

"This is Detective Inspector Rhymer speaking," Martin said. "I'm sorry to trouble you, but I'm making some inquiries concerning Mr. Starkey, and I thought you might be able to help me."

"About Ron?" There was deep disappointment in the voice. "I thought it must be him calling. I mean, so early and all, y'know—that's the sort of thing he does when he feels like it. Has something happened to him? Is he all right? I've been feeling frantic about him. Has he been in an accident?"

"Not that I know of," Martin answered, "but I'd like to talk to you if I may. May I come round to see you?"

"What, now?"

"If possible."

"It's just that I'm not dressed, y'know, and I haven't had breakfast and I have to be at work at nine o'clock, so I haven't got long. But if you don't mind that . . ."

"Will you tell me where you live? We found the note he made of your telephone number, but not your address."

"It's 57 Bathurst Place."

"I know it," Martin said. It was only a few minutes' walk away. "I'll be round almost at once, then."

He rang off, realising only after he had done so that he had forgotten to ask her name.

However, when he arrived at 57 Bathurst Place, he saw the name Jackie Nelson on a card beside one of the bells at the side of the door. Jackie Nelson lived in a block of flats which looked as if it had been built in the thirties. The walls were of white roughcast, the roof of green pantiles. There was a look of shabbiness about it, of cheap building. Martin rang the bell, then climbed three flights of stairs, coming face to face at the top of them with a girl who stood in an open doorway, waiting for him.

She was even younger than her voice had sounded on

the telephone. He thought that she could not be as much as twenty. She was small and rather plump, with long, straight fair hair draped about her shoulders, and she was wearing a kind of kaftan made of purple towelling. Her face was round and pink with a vague sort of friendliness about it. She was nursing an earthenware mug from which she took a sip as Martin came up the last few steps towards her.

"Would you like some tea?" she asked. "I've only just made it."

"Thank you," he said, "I should."

She led him into her room. It was a bed-sitting-room with an unmade divan bed against one wall and a cupboard door, standing open, showing clothes hanging from a rail. The room was very untidy, yet at some time a brave attempt had been made to brighten it up. There were red-and-white-striped curtains, a red carpet, a quantity of pot plants which it took Martin a moment to recognise as plastic, and some prints of lively abstract paintings. There was a tray with a teapot on it on a table by the window.

The girl went through a door that opened into a little kitchen as untidy as the bed-sitting-room and returned with a second mug. She poured out some tea and handed the mug to Martin, saying, "Help yourself to sugar and whatnot. And tell me what's happened. Is it something awful? Why do the police want Ron?"

"We're merely trying to discover his whereabouts," Martin said. "He vanished from his lodgings on Friday night. His landlady hasn't seen him since, and at her request I'm making these inquiries."

"That's Mrs. Winter, isn't it?" the girl said. "I've been thinking of telephoning her to ask her if she knew anything about him, but I don't know, I thought it might annoy him and I didn't want that. I mean, if it was simply that he'd finished with me, I didn't want him thinking I was trying to pester him. Actually, y'know, if he's finished with me, I've finished with him, that's what I'm like. But I couldn't help wondering if he'd been in an accident or got himself into trouble somehow."

"Trouble?" Martin said. "What kind of trouble?"

"Oh, I don't know, nothing special. He'd a funny way of talking sometimes, so you couldn't help wondering. Where his money came from, for instance. I always felt there was something queer about it. Why don't you sit down?" She tossed the covers of the bed roughly into place and sat down on it herself. "I told you I haven't got long, didn't I?"

Martin sat down on a low hammock-like chair.

"What's the job you've got to go to?"

"I'm a checker at the Co-op."

"The Co-op?" A sudden thought occurred to him. "If you're a checker, you work quite close to the windows, don't you?"

"That's right."

"You can see the street."

"I suppose so, when I've time."

"I wonder . . . Do you know Mrs. Legge? I think she's a regular customer."

The girl shook her head. "You don't get to know the customers in a place like that. You're too busy."

"Well, did you by any chance see Mr. Starkey on Saturday morning, carrying a parcel, go to a car parked just outside the shop and put the parcel inside it?"

"On a Saturday morning? You're joking. There are queues for us halfway down the shop."

"Yes, I see, of course there would be. I thought perhaps if you'd seen someone you knew go by, you might have noticed him."

"Well, I daresay I might have really, but I didn't."

"When did you see him last, then?"

"Last Thursday," she said. "We had dinner together, then he came back here for a time, then went back to Mrs. Winter's. Then on Friday I didn't see him because he was going to some ball or other, a charity do, y'know, dressed up in some silly gear. But I expected to see him on Saturday. I expected him round for lunch and I got a really nice couple of steaks and a nice ripe melon and a bottle of wine. It was just Spanish stuff, nothing special, but I thought he'd enjoy it. And he never came. But I didn't worry, because that's what he's like. I just put the things in the fridge and thought they'd do for the evening. But he didn't come then either, and I still didn't worry, because it doesn't pay to worry with someone like Ron. You've either got to put up with him the way he is or finish with him. And I'd really got quite fond of him, y'know, and I thought he cared just a bit for me. Oh well . . ." She gave a sigh. "I've eaten both the steaks now and they were fine, but generally I don't spend so much money on just myself, and I've nearly finished the melon, but I haven't opened the wine. That'll keep, in case he ever turns up again."

"Did he say anything on Thursday about the ball or about anything that might happen on the Friday evening?" Martin asked.

"Not really. He told me about his costume, but he seemed—I don't know how to put it—kind of depressed. Said it hadn't been any use coming here and he was thinking of moving on and how I'd been good to him but perhaps we'd have to say goodbye soon. And that's why I got the steaks and all, to show I didn't bear any malice. I'll make it like a kind of a celebration, I thought, something nice to remember, I'm not going to cry. I don't go in for crying much. And then he never came at all."

"Do you know of any friends he had besides yourself? I mean, people who might be able to tell us anything about him?"

"Only Sir Edward and Lady Guest. But I don't think he liked them much, they were just kind of relations."

"How long have you known him?"

"Oh, only a few weeks. He hasn't been here very long. We met one day in a café soon after he came to Pottershill. I can't say I ever got to know him very well. He told me a lot about himself, his travels, y'know, and his writing and so on, but I never knew how much to believe. He was always joking. You couldn't tell when he was serious. But like I said, I got quite fond of him. Mr. Rhymer, do you think something's happened to him?"

Martin was not sure whether, for the girl's sake, to hope that something had or that it hadn't. He had a feeling that she had been wasted on Ronald Starkey.

"I honestly don't know," he said. "But if by any chance he should get in touch with you, will you let me know?"

"All right."

Martin stood up. "Thank you for the tea. And for your help. I'll let you get off to that job of yours now."

Not that the girl had been able to help much, except to round out a little Martin's impression of Starkey. They had met a few times in Ruth's house, but only briefly, and Martin had never paid much attention to him. Now he realised that that was a pity. Ever since reading the letter to her brother from Caroline Guest, Martin had been worrying increasingly about Starkey's disappearance. A dangerous game, blackmail, if your intended victim turns out

to be as ruthless as you are yourself. Or even more ruthless still.

But was Edward Guest a ruthless man? What would a
man of his kind do if he was threatened with blackmail?
What kind of man was he?

That was the problem that Martin presently discussed
with Superintendent Nickerson, and the outcome of that
discussion was that Martin once more drove out to the
Guests' bungalow, but not alone this time. Sergeant Belling went with him. The time had come, the Superintendent thought, for making it plain that Martin's inquiry
was official. Jack Belling was a short, stout man about ten
years older than Martin, who thought he had done very
well to achieve the rank of sergeant and had no further
ambitions. He was a quiet, stolid man with the art of
making himself unobtrusive, which could be extremely
useful sometimes.

He hung back a little when Martin rang the Guests'
bell, yet when the door was opened by Edward Guest, his
gaze went straight past Martin to the sergeant, as Guest
obviously took in the significance of his presence there.

"Ah, Inspector, back again," Guest said. It was "Inspector" again, not "Martin." "Come in. I see you haven't
brought the dress back, but can you tell me anything
about its strange wanderings?"

There had been a change in Guest since Martin had
seen him last. He had lost the almost distracted air that
he had had the day before. His voice was crisp, his movements were precise and brisk. He took Martin and the
sergeant into the big, pleasant drawing room.

"I'm sorry, sir, I can't tell you how the dress got to the
Economy Centre," Martin said, "but I can tell you that
the blood on it is human blood and it's of the group O.
That happens to be your wife's blood group."

Guest did not appear disconcerted. Gesturing to chairs and sitting down himself, he even smiled.

"I didn't murder my wife, Inspector, if that's what you've come to discuss with me," he said. "I can't believe that anybody did. I'm sure I shall hear from her sooner or later. In fact, I imagine that if you were to publish in the newspapers a statement to the effect that I was suspected of her murder, she would get in touch with you at once to correct your error. She may not have been satisfied with our marriage, but she isn't malignant or wholly irresponsible. She wouldn't want to land me in serious trouble."

"We aren't in the habit of publishing facts like that," Martin said woodenly.

"Of course I realise that." Guest smiled again, as if it amused him to have been taken, apparently, so seriously. "You have no news of her, I suppose."

"I'm afraid not," Martin answered. "Nor of Mr. Starkey. Inquiries at hospitals and into road accidents have been begun, but we've found out nothing yet. It's Mr. Starkey we've come to talk about today."

"I've told you, I know nothing about his disappearance," Guest said. "I admit that the two of them, he and my wife, going away at the same time, must strike anyone who didn't know them as suspicious, but I'm as sure as it's possible to be in the circumstances that they didn't go together."

"Did she by any chance go in a car of yours?" Martin asked. "I don't think I asked you that before."

"No, both cars are in the garage."

"And Mr. Starkey's car is in its usual place in front of Mrs. Winter's house, and that suggests that even if they left together, it was in some third person's car. But what we've really come for is to show you a letter that Mrs.

Winter found in Mr. Starkey's room. I'd like to know if he ever showed it to you."

"Ah, *that* letter."

"Then you've seen it."

"No."

"Yet you know about it."

There was a note of sadness in Guest's voice. "Yes, I've been—shall we say, threatened with it?"

"By Mr. Starkey?"

"Of course."

"He told you what was in it?"

"Yes, and he offered to show me a copy of it. I told him it wasn't necessary. Do I strike you as a person it would be easy to blackmail, Inspector? I told him that if I heard another word about it from him I should go to the police."

"And would you really have done that?"

"Certainly. The only thing that restrained me at the time was my relationship with Starkey. For my wife's sake—my first wife's sake—I didn't want to get him into trouble if it could be avoided."

"Would you like to see the letter?" Martin asked. "I have it here."

Guest suddenly looked unsure of himself. "I—I'm not sure that I should. But—yes, I suppose I should, though I imagine it will be painful. Yes, then, if I may."

Martin took the letter out of his pocket and out of its envelope and put it into Guest's outstretched hand.

He read it slowly and his face became totally expressionless as he did so. When he came to the end, he started again at the beginning. At last, refolding the letter and handing it back to Martin, he said in a low voice, "Yes, I see."

"Is it what you expected?" Martin asked.

"Oh yes," Guest said. "My brother-in-law described its contents quite accurately. But you see, I knew of its existence even before he told me about it. And I've never had any reason to fear it. I suppose if he showed it around among my acquaintances, as he threatened to do, I might have suffered a certain amount of inconvenience. There are always people who like to believe the worst of one. They'd no doubt have withdrawn their friendship from me. But that wouldn't have disturbed me unduly. Such people are no loss. It's true I'd have been most unwilling, for personal reasons, to have produced the evidence that would have cleared me of the charges in that pathetic document, but I should never, in any circumstances, have paid Starkey for his silence."

"Weren't you helping him financially all the same?"

"Ah, that was quite another matter. Yes, I gave him a small amount of help when he arrived. That was simply because I knew Caroline would have wanted me to. I gave him about two hundred pounds altogether. But that stopped as soon as he threatened me with that letter. It was very ill-judged on his part."

"Did he tell you where he'd come from?"

"New Zealand, he said. Why? Wasn't that true?"

"It may not have been."

"I'm sorry I can't tell you anything definite. I didn't pay much attention when he talked about it. A person who tells as many lies as he does is basically uninteresting."

"This letter, sir," Martin said, looking down at it as he held it, "is there any chance, in your view, that it's a forgery?"

"Ah, no. I wish there were, but I'm certain there isn't."

"You mentioned evidence just now that would clear you of the charges in it."

"Yes. Well . . ." Guest hesitated. He shifted his gaze a

little, so that it went past Martin into some region remote from them both. Then he stood up. "I'll show you something that I've never shown to anyone except my wife, Leila. She was there with me when I found it and we discussed it at the time and we decided there was no need to show it to anyone, and since then I think that even she and I have never talked about it. Just a moment."

He crossed to the writing table in a corner of the room, opened one of its small drawers and drew out an envelope which he handed to Martin. On it was the one word, "Edward," in what looked like the same small, uneven scrawl as the letter that had been found in Ronald Starkey's room.

"It's a letter that Caroline left for me when she killed herself in Nairobi," Guest went on. "She left two letters, both addressed to me, but one was for me to show to the police, and in it she simply said that she was killing herself because she couldn't face her illness and that no one but herself was to blame. This was the other one and she meant it to be private, just between her and me. Go ahead and read it."

With the sudden sharp revulsion against his work that he sometimes felt if he found himself involved in occasions like this, when anguish, however tightly controlled, was only too evident, Martin took the letter out of its envelope and read it.

My darling Edward,

I have a terrible confession to make. A month ago, before you persuaded me to face my illness, I convinced myself that you were poisoning me. I knew you were in love with Leila and I don't think I really blamed you for it. I know I haven't been much of a wife lately. But I couldn't bear it and in a sort of madness I wrote to Ronnie and told him that you were trying to kill me. I don't think I really believed it even while I was writing it. I knew, whatever your feelings were for Leila, you'd never do me any harm. And I'm only confessing this to you now in case Ronnie ever tries to use that letter against you. We both know what he's like, but he can't resist. I'm sorry, oh, I'm so sorry, Edward, I ever wrote it. And thank you for all the happiness you've given me. I wish I'd given more to you. I'm sorry I'm taking this way out now, but I can't see much reason to go on living. I've never been any good to anyone. I must finish now because I'm beginning to feel queer. I think the stuff's starting to work. I hope so, though it frightens me. I love you very much. Goodbye.

Caroline.

Edward Guest stood over Martin while he was reading and, as soon as he had finished, reached for the letter and put it back into the drawer in the writing table from which he had taken it. As he turned back towards Martin his face was as expressionless as it had been while he had been reading his first wife's other letter.

"Of course, you can see that her death was in a sense my fault," he said. "But also you can see that Ronald Starkey had no power over me."

"No," Martin agreed.

"I had no reason to go in fear of him."

"No."

"I had no reason ever to consider paying him blackmail."

"No."

"And so no reason to murder him, except in the unlikely event that he made off with my second wife, and as I've said to you, I think we can discount that."

"So it would seem."

Martin stood up. Sergeant Belling stood up beside him.

"I'm sorry I can't help you with any explanation of how my wife's dress got to the Economy Centre," Guest added as he showed them to the door, "but no doubt you'll solve that little mystery somehow. And when you're satisfied that you have, you and Ingrid really must come and have dinner with me sometime. I'll look forward to knowing you better."

CHAPTER 6

Ingrid spent that morning cleaning the house, doing some shopping and preparing lunch for Ruth and herself. Ruth was feeling better and her temperature had come down a little, signs of recovery which she attributed entirely to not having allowed any doctor to give her any pills. After lunch Ingrid went out in the Mini and inspected the houses of which she had shown Martin the particulars the evening before. Only one attracted her in the least and that was not a house but a flat, the ground floor of a solid Victorian mansion which stood in about an acre of garden. What she liked about the flat were the big rooms with walls thick enough to insure some degree of soundproofing, the lawns and the tall old trees that the windows overlooked, the quiet street outside, lined with chestnuts, which led nowhere except to this house, and the gentle little old woman who had been living in the flat for thirty years and who seemed to take a warm liking to Ingrid.

Not that the old woman went with the flat, but a quarter of the garden did and so did a good garage, and the price was not prohibitive. As Ingrid was leaving, the small, ancient owner said to her that she might even consider bringing it down a little if Ingrid felt tempted.

"So many people one takes round are so rude, you know," the little woman said. "They forget that one's showing them one's home—I mean, a place that one's cared about for a great deal of one's life—and they sneer at everything, even one's furniture, in a quite horrid way, just to try to cheapen it. They're the ones I always tell I've already had a very good offer. Then, there are the people who flutter round in a great hurry, say how perfectly lovely everything is and that they'll think about it, and naturally one never hears from them again. But you've looked at things very carefully and I've seen you thinking seriously about whether or not it would suit you, and you've been nice and polite without any of that silly, insincere overpraising. Well, don't try to make up your mind in a hurry. Go away and think about it. After all, one doesn't buy a house every day of the week. And if you like, I'll let you know if I have any offers, in case you've decided to put one in yourself, but I don't expect there'll be anything at once, because of course by modern standards it needs so many things done to it."

Describing the flat to Ruth a little later, Ingrid said, "And it does need a lot done to it, I'm afraid. For one thing, it's fearfully shabby and needs redecorating right through. But perhaps Martin and I could do most of that ourselves, so it wouldn't cost too much. Then the kitchen would simply have to be modernized, but it's a good shape and one could make it very nice. I think the bathroom would just do as it is if one repainted it. Anyway, I liked the place better than anything else I've looked at so far. Only I'm not sure how Martin's going to feel about the idea of a flat."

"If you've taken to it yourself," Ruth said from among her pillows, "and I think you have, I'd put a little pressure on him for once. Actually, I think he might be rather glad if you made his mind up for him. Of course I've been thinking that now that Ronald's gone and it looks as if he isn't coming back, there'd be room for you both here while you go on hunting. But I don't think it would really be a very good idea. You aren't going to want a mother-in-law under your feet when you first get married. You'd be far better advised to move into his lodgings. I haven't wanted to interfere, but I've often wondered why you didn't do that."

"Because it's one of the things Martin's stubborn about," Ingrid answered. "He won't have it. And of course I know why, though I'm not sure if he does. He thinks it's because of the kitchen and bathroom and so on, but really it's because of the other women he's taken there at various times. It's a bit difficult really, but I've got to be absolutely different from all of them. He's made up his mind our getting married has got to be a completely new beginning for us both." She gazed away out of the window. "I wonder if it will be."

"I shouldn't worry too much if it isn't," Ruth said. "The only new beginning you get is your birth, and to all appearances that's expremely unpleasant. I don't believe anyone enjoys it. I'm sure one's better off when one's got loaded up with a reasonable amount of baggage from the past. Is Marting coming in this evening?"

"If he can."

He had telephoned soon after his visit to Edward Guest and told Ingrid most of what had happened between them. She had handed this information on to Ruth, who had looked absent and not said much about it.

"If he does come," she said, "you could take him straight out to see your old woman and her flat, couldn't you?"

"Only I think it would be better for him to see it by daylight. He'd see the garden then. And I expect he'll be tired when he gets here and not in too good a mood for taking a liking to anything."

Ruth smiled. "You really do want that place, don't you? Well, go ahead and be firm with him."

Ingrid looked at her watch. It was a quarter past five.

"I think I'll just pop out to the shops again," she said. "I want to pick up a bottle of whisky for you. We're getting a bit low with all those hot drinks you've been having. And we need some lemons. I shan't be long. I'll be back before Martin gets here."

She set off in the Mini, though not in the first instance to buy the whisky, but having an itch to find out if anyone else was interested in the flat, she called in at Fordham and Knowle's, the house agents. Yet when the young man she spoke to in the office asked her if she had seen anything she fancied, she suddenly felt unable to say anything about it. She was aware that there was something superstitious about her silence, a feeling that if she allowed herself to state openly she had seen something that she wanted—even, she was beginning to think, wanted very much indeed—it would be snatched away from her. She said that she had called in to see if any new properties had come on to the market, and when she was told that there was nothing that would interest her, went out into the gathering dusk, bought the whisky and the lemons that she wanted and walked towards the car park.

Ahead of her she noticed a familiar figure. She saw the tall, well-built body, the little head of Andrew Legge, who had just emerged from his office and was also walking towards the car park.

As he was unlocking his car, he saw her and called out, "Hallo, Ingrid. Nice to see you. How's Ruth?"

Ingrid thought of her glimpse of Sandra the evening before and of Martin's advice that Ingrid should give her some warning about the character of the boy who had been with her. But that did not mean warning Sandra's father.

"Beginning to recover, I think," she answered.

"Good, good," he said. "You haven't seen Mrs. Belcher, I suppose."

"No," Ingrid said, wondering wildly for a moment if May Belcher was to be added to the list of people who had disappeared. "Not since Saturday morning."

"Dreadful woman," Andrew Legge went on. "Frightful gossip. Spreading rumours. Quite untrue."

"Oh, about that dress, you mean, that Mrs. Legge brought in to the Economy Centre," Ingrid said.

"No, no, that's just some bit of nonsense," he said. "Someone played a trick on Stephanie to get her into trouble with the rest of you. I don't know how it was done, but it isn't important. No, the Belcher woman's been spreading the rumour that Leila's left Edward. I wondered if Ruth had heard."

"She hasn't heard anything from Mrs. Belcher," she said cautiously.

"She will, she will," he said, "as soon as she's well enough to go back to the Centre. The place is a hive of gossip. Stephanie's thinking of breaking her connection with it. She says no one there ever talks of anything even reasonably intelligent, and since this trick's been played on her, she says people are beginning to look at her in an odd way. That may be just her imagination, of course. She's got a great deal of imagination. I keep telling her she ought to write a book. Well, well, give Ruth my best wishes. I hope she feels better soon."

He got into his car.

Ingrid got into the Mini and drove home.

In the kitchen she lit the oven to heat it up for the leg

of lamb that she was going to cook, peeled some potatoes, washed a cauliflower and put a slightly disspirited-looking fruit flan that she had bought that morning onto a plate. She whipped some cream to cheer up the flan, put a tray ready for Ruth and laid the table in the dining room for herself and Martin.

He arrived just after she had put the lamb and the potatoes into the oven. She suggested that they should take their drinks upstairs to keep Ruth company for a little, and the two of them went up to her room, carrying their drinks. She told them that this staying in bed was nonsense and that she had intended to come downstairs for dinner, but Ingrid told her that she was not even to think of doing such a thing yet, then described her meeting with Andrew Legge.

"So Edward's told May about Leila leaving him," Ruth said thoughtfully as she sipped her drink, "and May's spreading it around. I suppose that was bound to happen sooner or later and it doesn't actually matter in the least. But I wonder why Edward told May. He must have known she'd talk and he's the kind of person who really suffers if that happens. His dignity's so enormously important to him. He must have gone to pieces worse than I'd have thought."

"He seemed to me to have got control of himself far better today than yesterday," Martin said. "That letter of Starkey's you found didn't upset him at all, and he convinced me Starkey had nothing to blackmail him with. Incidentally, he convinced me pretty well that no one could blackmail him. He's the kind of person who'd think that going to the police was the only normal thing to do about a blackmailer. He'd be very difficult to intimidate. And he convinced me that it's very unlikely that Starkey and his wife went off together. But it looks as if Guest isn't the only person who could have a motive for wanting to get rid of Starkey. We've been finding out some rather interesting things about him today."

"From that address book?" Ingrid asked.

Martin nodded. "Jack Belling's been on the telephone all the afternoon. Most of the people he contacted were very reserved and said Starkey was just a casual acquaintance whom they hadn't seen for a year or two, but one or two let fly and said that if Starkey had been to the police about them in spite of what they'd paid him, they'd tell the police anything they wanted to know about Starkey. How it looks is that he's been a small-time blackmailer for some years. Mostly he's preyed on people who've committed sexual offences. They're the easiest to catch out, of course. But he came up against one tough character and got himself into deep water and did a stretch of two years. When he came out he tried living off his sister in Hertfordshire, then, when he was kicked out from there, he came on here to get what he could out of Guest. At first, according to Guest, he helped him with one or two loans, but that stopped the moment Starkey tried to put pressure on him with his sister's letter."

"What do you think?" Ingrid asked. "That one of his victims traced him down here and killed him?"

"We've no evidence at all that he's dead," Martin said. "I think it's more likely that someone threatened him with exposure or danger of some sort and he's found it convenient to disappear."

"Leaving his car?" Ruth said. "Why didn't he go in it?"

"Too easy to trace. Taking a small suitcase with a few clothes in it and going off by train would be much less conspicuous. You aren't sure, are you, Ruth, that he didn't take some clothes with him?"

"No. But all the same . . ." She interrupted herself with

an attack of sneezing. "Damn this disease!" she said as it
subsided. "I thought I was nearly over it. But colds always seem to get worse towards evening, don't they? I
was going to say, Martin, whatever Edward says, I think
Ronald and Leila must have gone off together. Or that
their going away at the same time is connected in some
way. I wonder if he could have been blackmailing her for
something. She might not be nearly as strong-minded
about it as Edward. And there's the possibility that the
man she went off with, if it wasn't Ronald, turned on him
and frightened him off, or even killed him. What about
that, Martin?"

"It's about the best suggestion anyone's come up with
so far," he answered. "You're quite a detective."

"Now you're laughing at me," she said, "but I'm not
completely stupid. I do have some good ideas."

"You have too many of them, that's the trouble," Ingrid
said. She finished her sherry. "Just a minute now. I must
go and look at the potatoes. Don't have too many more
ideas while I'm gone."

She went downstairs to the kitchen.

Presently, when she and Martin were eating roast lamb
in the dining room, she told him about the flat that she
had seen in the afternoon. As she talked about it, she discovered that she was even more enthusiastic about it than
she had realised while she was being shown over it. He
listened with less than his usual attentiveness. He nodded
and agreed with everything that she said about the charm
of big rooms and good, solid building and the attrac-
tiveness of having several great old trees in your garden
and the pleasantness of living in such a quiet part of the
town. Even when Ingrid talked about the mortgage that
they would have to raise, he seemed to feel no qualms.

Almost his only comment was when Ingrid told him that she really felt that the owner had taken a liking to her and would feel that her beloved old home was in good hands if she and Martin bought it.

"Quite a saleswoman, your little old lady," he remarked.

"Oh, but I really think she meant it," Ingrid said. "Martin, what's the matter? You haven't been listening to anything I've been saying."

"I'm sorry," he said. "It's true. I've got something on my mind. I'm haunted by something, but I don't know what it is."

"Something about these disappearances?"

"Yes. Something that may be important. I think it's something someone said. Guest, I believe. Either this morning or yesterday. And I half noticed it at the time and began to think about it, then we went straight on talking about something else and I lost it."

"Was it something he said that made you think he knows more about what's happened than he's been saying?"

"Not necessarily. It was just something he said—I think it must have been Guest I'm thinking of—that started up some idea in my brain, but it's no good, I've lost it."

"Don't think about it, then. That's always best. You'll find it'll come back suddenly when you don't expect it. Now, shall I tell you about my lovely flat all over again?"

"Go ahead," he said with a smile.

She started to repeat all that she had said before. They spent a quiet, comfortable evening together, an evening of tenderness and peace. This was an atmosphere, Ingrid realised, that was unfamiliar to Martin, but that he deeply needed to experience. By the end of the evening the flat was not only theirs in imagination, but was decorated and furnished, with carefully chosen curtains at the tall windows and even had daffodils coming into bloom under the trees in the garden.

The next morning, about seven o'clock, while Ingrid was still in a deep sleep, her door was softly opened and Ruth came in, carrying a cup of tea. She hesitated when she saw how soundly asleep Ingrid was, but then could not restrain herself. Putting the teacup down on the bedside table, she gave Ingrid's shoulder a gentle shake.

"Darling," Ruth said, "listen to me. I've been thinking."

Ingrid stirred and opened her eyes.

"You've been at it again," she said. "If you want tea, why don't you let me get it?"

"You were asleep and I've been lying awake for hours. And I'm sure I've thought of something important."

"Well, go back to bed and don't catch cold. I'll come to your room and you can tell me about it."

"D'you know, you often talk to me as if I were a child?" Ruth said. "I'm quite all right. I'm much better. Listen, Ingrid." She perched on the edge of the bed. "You remember telling Martin and me yesterday how Andrew told you May Belcher's been spreading it around that Leila's left Edward?"

Ingrid pulled herself up in the bed and reached for the teacup. She realised that she did often treat her mother as if she were a child, but how could she help it?

"Of course," she said.

"And I said that I wondered why Edward had told May about it, that it didn't seem like him."

"Yes."

"Well, the reason's obvious and it's given me an idea."

"Go on."

"It's just that Edward didn't tell May about it at all. But you see, May's about the nearest thing to a friend

Leila's got in Pottershill. I don't know why she liked her
specially. They're completely different. But there's something rather imposing about May and I think perhaps she
impressed Leila. So if May knows that Leila's left Edward, I don't think it's because Edward's said anything to
her, I think it's because Leila's been in touch with her."

"You've decided she's alive, then."

"Why not?"

"That dress—"

"Look, that dress was a joke of Ronald's, I thought we'd
decided that. But what I thought is that you might go
along to see May this morning. I know she won't be at the
Centre today, she'll be at home, so you can easily keep
things confidential, and you can ask her if at least she can
tell you if Leila's alive. And she might even tell you more
than that if you go about it the right way."

"She hardly knows me," Ingrid protested.

"But it's worth trying, isn't it?"

"What's the point of it if you're so sure Lady Guest's
alive?"

"Oh, darling, if you don't *want* to . . ."

"I don't want to the least little bit, but I suppose I'll
have to."

It was about ten o'clock when Ingrid set off for May
Belcher's house. It was on the outer edge of the town and,
in the days before the suburbs had engulfed it, had been
a small farmhouse. It was built of stone, with its windows
set deep in thick walls and a roof of silvery grey slates. To
right and left of it were Edwardian mansions, mostly
divided into flats, with a look of brash opulence about
them. Compared with them, the little house had an air of
sober dignity which matched May's personality very well.

She opened the door to Ingrid, took her into the drawing room, asked the usual questions about Ruth's flu and

offered her tea. Declining it, Ingrid settled among a quantity of embroidered cushions on a flower-patterned sofa, began by apologising for having come at all, then, because she did not know how to approach the subject, went straight to the point.

"Actually, I came because my mother's been wondering if Lady Guest has been in touch with you," she said.

"Leila?" May said, looking surprised. "No, I haven't seen her since the ball."

"Or Sir Edward?"

"No. Why?"

"Well, we've been worried about Lady Guest ever since that dress turned up with the bloodstains and the bullet hole, and nobody's seen her. Then yesterday Mr. Legge told me that Mrs. Legge had heard from you that Lady Guest had left Sir Edward, so my mother thought that if you really knew something about her, I mean, if perhaps you'd heard from her since she went away, it would at least mean she's alive and that would be a relief."

"That woman Stephanie!" May exploded. "Honestly, Ingrid, the way she twists things! I never said a word about Leila having left Edward. Mind you, for all I know, she may have, and if she has I've an uncomfortable feeling that I'm partly to blame, though of course that's ridiculous." To blame her for anything, May seemed to imply, would always be ridiculous. "No, what I actually said was that it was far more likely that Leila had left Edward than that he'd shot and killed her. And what's wrong with saying that? I only said it to make that silly little Sykes girl stop saying he'd murdered her. She kept saying that the police—she meant your Martin—had come in and taken Leila's dress away and it was clear as day they thought it was a case of murder. And so I simply told her she was talking rubbish and that she'd a horrid little mind and that I'd sooner believe Leila had gone off with some man than that she was dead. That's really all I said. And look what Stephanie's made of it."

"Then, you haven't heard anything from Lady Guest herself," Ingrid said.

"Not a word. I wish I had."

"Nor from Sir Edward?"

"Oh, he wouldn't talk about a thing like that to me," May said. "We don't know each other particularly well."

"Actually, I don't think Martin believes Sir Edward killed Lady Guest," Ingrid said. "Clare Sykes got it all wrong."

"Of course she did. Even if someone else did. Oh goodness—" May clapped her hand to her mouth. "I shouldn't have said that. I'm almost as bad as she is. It's just because of that dress. It *does* take a bit of explaining. No, Ingrid dear, what I really think has happened to Leila is that she's gone away with a nephew of mine, Nigel Brooke. That's why I have this absurd sort of guilty feeling. I never meant to, but I almost threw them together. Did you meet Nigel when he was down here in the summer? He stayed with me for several weeks. I was so pleased at the time. He generally comes down for just a weekend now and then, but this summer he kept asking if he could stay on for a little while longer and told me how restful it felt to be here and how much good it was doing him. And silly old me, I was delighted. I've always been very fond of him, but I've always thought his visits to me were just a kind of duty and that they rather bored him. He mixes with much more exciting people than I can introduce him to here. I've never quite understood what his job is, but it's something to do with making advertising films and he meets lots of beautiful women and makes lots of money. When he's here he spends most of his time playing golf. And that's how it began, you see, because I thought it would be nice for him to meet the Guests, who hadn't come here yet when he stayed with me last. And they seemed to get on so well. Oh dear, I do hate this responsible feeling! But now mind, Ingrid, you won't say a word of any of this to anyone but Ruth, will you? Promise?"

"But you know the police are looking for Lady Guest," Ingrid answered. "If you told them this it might save them a lot of trouble."

"But I may be quite wrong," May protested quickly. "Nigel may not come into the picture at all."

"Have you thought of getting in touch with him to ask him if he's seen Lady Guest?" Ingrid asked.

"As a matter of fact, I have. At the risk of seeming a busybody, when I couldn't get in touch with Leila here, I rang him up and he told me in rather less than his usual charming way to mind my own business. He didn't take my inquiries at all well."

"Won't you tell me his address so that I can tell it to Martin? I won't tell a soul but Martin," Ingrid promised.

May looked as if she were going to refuse, then she shrugged her shoulders.

"They'll find it out anyway, I suppose," she said and told Ingrid an address in Westminster. "But tell them I don't guarantee for a moment they'll find Leila there. It's just an idea I had."

Ingrid nodded, made a note of the address and left soon afterwards.

She did not drive straight home. She found herself in a disturbing mood of depression. It had suddenly come over her while she was talking to May Belcher that nearly all the marriages she knew of were unhappy. Or was she exaggerating because she had been so saturated during the last few days in the problems of Edward Guest's two unfortunate marriages?

So far as she knew, her parents' marriage had been happy, though tragically brief, but take the Legges, for instance. They could hardly be said to love one another dearly. And someone or other, Ingrid remembered, had told her that May Belcher's husband had been the most appalling bore and that she got far more out of life now that she was a widow. And Clare Sykes, after only a few months of marriage, was very restive.

Most of Ingrid's friends in her own generation who had married seemed to be doing well enough, but their relationships had not yet been tested by time, and wasn't it only because of time, because of the long vista of the future, that marriage was important? Why marry at all if in ten years' time, in twenty years, you were not going to be even more in love than you were at present? But how that thought could scare you if you let yourself dwell on it.

She tried to telephone Martin from a call box to tell him what she had been told by May Belcher, but was told that he was not available as he was giving evidence in court that morning. She yielded then to an impulse to drive out into the country. The day was sunny, though there was a cold wind blowing. White puffs of cloud chased each other skittishly across the sky. The winds of the last few days had torn most of the leaves from the trees, except in sheltered hollows. There they still glowed, golden and russet. The hawthorn hedges were smothered in red berries.

Returning after about an hour of aimless driving, she found herself passing the end of the street that led nowhere except to the house that she had visited the day before, with the ground-floor flat in it that had been at the back of her mind ever since. Accident? Or was this what she had intended ever since she had set out that morning? She turned the car into the avenue of chestnuts and stopped at the gate of the big house.

The little old woman came slowly to answer her ring at the bell. She turned out to be even older than Ingrid had realised yesterday, but the impression of smallness that she gave was at least partly due to the curve of her spine. When she had been able to stand upright she had probably been as tall as Ingrid. She was wearing a well-cut tweed skirt and a cashmere twin-set. She looked up at Ingrid with a sparkling smile.

"You know, I thought you'd be back," she said. "But where is your husband? Doesn't he want to take a look round too?"

"He's too busy to come just now," Ingrid answered. "And actually we aren't married yet, though we shall be quite soon. I'll bring him along, if I may, as soon as he's got some time to spare. But I thought if I could look round again, I could tell more about the flat, because there are a few things I can't remember."

"That's a very good idea," the old woman said. "And I think it would be best if you just look round by yourself. Look anywhere you like and take as long as you like about it. You'll find the back door's unlocked, so you can walk straight out into the garden. And when you've seen all you want to, perhaps you'll join me for a drink. Will you give me that pleasure? I enjoy a drink, but I'm very strict with myself about drinking alone. I never do it. I've seen so many lonely old women get into the habit of having a little nip whenever they happen to feel like it and end up in a very sad state. I shouldn't like that to happen to me. Now go ahead and join me in the drawing room when you're ready."

She turned and tottered off slowly into one of the big rooms.

Ingrid joined her there about twenty minutes later. She had wandered round the flat in a vague dream, seeing the excellent but ancient and discoloured wallpaper replaced by pearl-grey paint and the sombre velvet curtains by vivid linens and the good furniture that Martin had in his lodgings placed very carefully here and there to show it off at its best and the kitchen painted a clear, bright yellow instead of dingy cream, with all the shining gadgetry that has come to seem essential to modern living.

The only thing to which Ingrid had given no thought was the cost of the flat, for if you wanted a thing enough, surely you could get it somehow.

The old woman, who said that she was Mrs. Aitken, said apologetically that she could only offer her gin and tonic or some long-opened sherry which she did not recommend. Ingrid chose the gin and tonic, but was slightly taken aback when she tried it, for Mrs. Aitken believed in making a drink very strong. She settled Ingrid in a deep armchair, but herself sat on one that was stiff and high, explaining that she found it easier at her age to get out of a chair of that kind than one that looked more comfortable.

Beaming gently at Ingrid, she said with pride, "I'm nearly ninety." Then she lifted her glass and said, "Cheers."

Ingrid echoed her and sipped cautiously at the potent drink that she had been given.

"You know, I'd like to think of someone young coming to live here again," Mrs. Aitken went on. "My husband and I were quite young when we came here first. He was just out of the army after the war and I was a nurse. We met in the hospital where they sent him when he was wounded. I'm talking about the first war, of course. I don't suppose you know anything about it. You probably don't even know much about the second. I find that so hard to realise, I mean that there's a whole generation of quite mature young people whose lives haven't been marked by those wars, as ours were. Wonderful to think of, in a way, except that the world seems in as much of a mess as ever. Well, we bought this house—the whole house, you know—you could pick up big houses like this for a song at the time, and this one was in particularly bad condition because it had been used as a hostel for Belgian refugees. The things they'd done to it! I suppose displaced people always behave oddly, they feel so dreadful about everything. So we got it really cheap and we got it all cleaned up gradually and we had a cook and two maids and a full-time gardener. Just think of it!" She gave a little crow of laughter. "And we weren't even rich. Our cook used to intimidate us terribly because she insisted on being called by her surname, Collins. She wouldn't allow us to call her Mrs. Collins, she seemed to think it would lower her professional status. How extraordinary it seems now. My husband was an engineer. He worked for the firm of Grant and Spicer. You wouldn't know about them, they're long since defunct, but they were a very good firm in their day. Oh dear, I'm talking too much. I don't often have the chance of talking to such a good listener. Let me top up your drink."

"No, thank you," Ingrid said quickly. "I've got to drive home."

"Ah yes, you've a car," Mrs. Aitken said. "We'd no car, you know, until years later. My husband used to walk to his work every day. And we had three children. This was a lovely house for children. I remember, just about this time of year, they'd collect the conkers from the chestnuts outside and play quite alarming games with them. But they all grew up and married and one lives in London and one in Glasgow and one in New York. And when they'd all gone my husband and I decided to split the house up into flats and keep just this one for ourselves. That was soon after the end of the second war. But we were careful to keep it big enough for the children to be able to come to stay with us. And after a bit they started bringing their children and now there are great-grandchildren too. Oh yes!" She nodded and smiled happily. "I've got twelve great-grandchildren. I've never seen several of them, but I've got lovely photographs of them all."

"Where are you going when you leave here?" Ingrid asked.

"I'm going to live with my sister in Bournemouth," Mrs. Aitken answered. "She's got a very nice little flat in a modern block with a lift and such a nice porter, she says, who changes her electric light bulbs for her and hangs up the clean curtains and does all those jobs that it gets difficult to do when you're old, and she's got a nice daily help too and we've always got on very well together. I think it should work. I've really found this place too much to manage since my husband died, even though I've an excellent daily. Besides, the children don't think I ought to live by myself any more. My husband had a stroke, poor man, a year ago, and then almost immediately another, and that killed him. A mercy, in a way, that it was so quick, because he'd always been very active, and if he hadn't been able to move around easily and talk normally it would have driven him out of his mind. But I miss him terribly. We used to do everything together. When he retired he even began to take an interest in cooking and

used to do the shopping for me and help in all kinds of
ways. So I really shouldn't complain, should I? We had a
wonderful life. If you come to live here you'll find it's a
happy house. Perhaps you don't agree with me, but I
think you can tell about houses. They seem to live lives of
their own, and some are somehow doomed and nobody
ever stays in them and others make you love them and become a part of you. Or is that all superstition, do you
think?"

"I don't know," Ingrid said. "I haven't had time to find
out yet."

She finished her drink and stood up. She did feel something welcoming and cheerful in the shabby old flat, but
for the present at least she was inclined to attribute it to
its owner's contentment of mind, her thankfulness for all
the joys of her long life and perhaps a little to her gin.

"I'll bring Martin along as soon as I can," she said.

On her way home she found that her depression had
evaporated. The feeling that she had had earlier in the
morning that marriage was almost certain to turn out dis-
astrously had gone. It might be as wonderful as you
hoped. She was humming a soft, meaningless little tune to
herself when she reached home and let herself in at the
door.

She heard voices in the living room. So Ruth had got
up again, instead of staying in bed as she should have.
One voice was hers. Ingrid did not immediately recognise
the other. But as soon as she opened the door she remembered it and felt a sudden chill. It was absurd to feel such
a thing, but for an instant it was as if she were listening to
some ghost speaking.

"What I'd like to know is whether you think Edward
would like me to come back to him," Leila Guest was saying. "You know him better than anybody."

CHAPTER 7

It was only as she listened to that voice that Ingrid
realised to what extent she had been taking for granted
that Leila Guest was dead, that she had been killed wearing her beautiful pink ball dress, however strange the
subsequent wanderings of the dress might be. But why,
then, should the sound of her voice not cause simple relief, instead of that spasm of fear, as if her being alive
were something uncanny?

When Ingrid appeared in the doorway of the living
room, Leila Guest was standing by the window with the
look of having just paused there for a moment from roam-
ing restlessly about the room. She was a very slim woman
about the same height as Ingrid, though the way her
beautifully modelled head was held high on a slender
neck made her look taller than she was. Her hair was ash-
blond and was cropped very short. Its colour, which
Ingrid believed was its own, contrasted arrestingly with
the darkness of her eyes and with her long, dark lashes.
She had a small face with features which perhaps in a few
years' time would begin to look a little sharp, but which
at present had a delicate, birdlike charm. If there was
anything wrong with it, it was that it was an arrogant
face, too full of self-assurance. There was no softness in it.
She was accustomed to see admiration in any eyes that
met hers, and accepted this as merely normal. Today she
was wearing a light-green dress, simple and certainly very

expensive, and had very little make-up on her pale, perfect skin. A short mink jacket had been tossed down on a chair.

Ruth, who was sitting close to the gas fire, was in her old blue dressing-gown and slippers, and her greying hair looked as if it had not been brushed that morning. The arrival of Leila Guest must have taken her by surprise.

Leila said, "Hallo, Ingrid, Ruth's been telling me how your policeman has all but insisted on digging up poor Edward's garden, looking for my corpse. If I'd known anything about it, I'd have let him know it wasn't necessary. Edward himself knew it wasn't necessary. He had my note, telling him I'd get in touch with him as soon as I'd made up my mind what I was going to do. But I suppose none of you believed him if he told you about it. It must have been much more exciting to think he was a murderer."

"Well, there was the funny problem of the dress with the bloodstains that somehow got into the Legges' car," Ingrid said, sitting down beside Ruth. "That was what started everyone worrying about you and which no one's explained yet."

"I don't know anything about the dress," Leila said. "I took it off as soon as I got home because it was so tight I could hardly breathe in it and I just dropped it somewhere and got dressed again and wrote that note for Edward and waited for Nigel to pick me up. Nigel Brooke. A nephew of May Belcher's. He was down here in the summer, d'you remember? And our idea was that we'd try things out for a little, then if they worked out well, ask Edward for a divorce and get married. But after a weekend of Nigel, I'm inclined to think I may have made a mistake. He's very good company, but he's also vain and selfish. I can't think why I didn't notice it before. Anyway, I came down to see Ruth to ask her how Edward's been taking things and whether or not she thinks he'd be glad if I came back to him. And I find she hasn't even seen him since I went away."

There was a note almost of accusation in Leila's voice.

Ruth responded meekly, "I haven't been out of the house since then. I haven't been seeing anyone."

"I know, I know." Leila made a gesture as if she were brushing aside a not very convincing excuse. "But then you come up with that extraordinary story about the dress. I can't understand it at all. Do you think Edward can have gone out of his mind when he found that note of mine and started pumping bullets into the dress because he couldn't get at me? He's got a gun, you know. He always had one in the house when he was in Tondolo and kept it."

"That doesn't account for the bloodstains," Ingrid said.

"I suppose not. Of course, Edward's been behaving in a very odd way for some time," Leila went on. "He's been terribly difficult. He got it into his head for some reason that I was turning into an alcoholic. We had some fearful rows about it, and really it was all because he was drinking far more himself than he realised. Our whisky kept vanishing and he'd flatly deny he'd had any of it. It was so strange, it rather frightened me, because he's normally an extremely truthful person. He's very intolerant of people who tell lies, like that wretched little brother-in-law of his. Not that Edward didn't let Ronald get away with a good deal more than I thought he ought to. When he arrived here broke, Edward gave him about two hundred pounds straightaway. He's a generous man. I've never criticised him for being mean."

"If there's a secret drinker in your house," Ruth said, "isn't it probably your Mrs. What's-her-name—that woman who cleans for you?"

"Mrs. Baldwin? Oh no, that's quite impossible." Leila

crossed the room towards the fireplace and sat down in a chair near it, crossing her perfect legs. "I did think of her at first, as a matter of fact, but she's dead honest, she really is, and the soul of sobriety. No, the trouble is just Edward himself. Retirement's been terribly bad for him. He's frustrated and bored. It's changed him very much in all kinds of ways. And d'you know, when he loses his temper, he's rather frightening. I don't suppose you've ever seen it. He puts on an air of icy dignity, when you know he's seething inside. I've been very near to leaving him all this past year, but until I met Nigel—well, I didn't want to go back to leading my old sort of life. I'm getting past the age when being the perfect secretary to some puffed-up shot has much glamour to it. Not that anyone could call life here very glamourous, could they?" Leila gave a bitter little laugh. "I've never made any real friends here. Nobody likes me. You've been nice to me, Ruth, but that's only been for Edward's sake. The truth is, I've found life hell in this blasted place."

Ruth's face, pale and drawn from her illness, took on a crumpled look of distress.

"Don't talk like that," she said. "I'm sure you can make your peace with Edward and come back if you want to. And there are lots of people here who admire you immensely."

"Oh, there are people who envy me, of course," Leila said indifferently. "But envy doesn't make them like you. Take that Legge woman, for instance, living right next door to us. How she hates me. Yet I've never done a thing to harm her. I've done my best to be nice to that witless child of hers and I've taken pains to get on well with her dreary husband. Yet the other day, when she came to pick up a few things I was sending to your Economy Centre, I swear to you I saw sheer murder in her face. Do you know how horrible it feels to be hated, Ruth? Has anyone ever hated you?"

"I don't think so. Not that I know of." Ruth stirred uneasily. "But I'm sure you're wrong about it, Leila. Stephanie doesn't hate you, it's just that she thinks you despise her. She's terribly sensitive."

Ingrid was far from agreeing with Ruth, but saw no virtue in saying so.

"Lady Guest," she said, "do you know anything about where Ronald Starkey meant to go after he took you home?"

Leila Guest gave a slight start, as if she was surprised to find Ingrid still in the room with her and Ruth.

"He didn't go anywhere," Leila said. "He said he wanted to talk to Edward, so I got him a drink and left him there. I don't know if he actually waited for Edward or got tired of it and came home."

"He didn't come home," Ruth said. "He hasn't been seen since that evening."

"Well, I can't tell you anything about that," Leila said. "When I left with Nigel, Ronald was sitting comfortably in the drawing room with his feet up and a glass of whisky to keep him going, looking perfectly revolting in that ridiculous little-girl's outfit he was wearing, with his knobby knees and hairy legs, but quite pleased with himself. I can't tell you for certain why he wanted to see Edward, but he'd dropped a hint to me that he thought Edward might give him some more money if he'd promise to go away. He came here, you know, with the idea of blackmailing Edward with some story about his having been involved in Caroline's death. Naturally, it didn't work. But I don't really know much about it."

"In that case," Ingrid remarked thoughtfully, "you seem to have been the last person hereabouts to have seen Ronald."

Leila gave her a long look, her eyebrows lifting.

"What's that supposed to mean, Ingrid?" she asked.

"I don't know," Ingrid said. "It's just something that struck me."

"Am I supposed to have made away with Ronald somehow? Can you tell me why I should have done such a thing, apart from the fact, which I shouldn't dream of denying, that I detested the little rat?"

"Of course Ingrid didn't mean that," Ruth said quickly.

"Oh, but why 'of course'?" Leila demanded. "I believe it's *just* what she meant. Didn't you think, Ingrid, that Ronald might have tried his blackmailing tricks on me? Let's not bother for the moment about what hold he might have had on me. But mightn't I have shot him with Edward's gun and got Nigel to carry his body out to the car for me? Then of course we'd have dumped it somewhere on the way to London. What theory could be more reasonable? I find it very convincing. I'm a very reasonable woman, you know. Whatever anyone's ever said against me, I honestly don't think they've been able to say I'm unreasonable."

"You aren't being very reasonable now," Ruth said. "Ingrid just dropped a remark—"

"But those little remarks people drop," Leila interrupted her, "they mean so much. They give away what's really in their minds. Don't they, Ingrid? Weren't you thinking more or less what I've just said?"

"Perhaps I was," Ingrid agreed.

"You see, she's more honest than you are, Ruth," Leila said. "But I'll tell you something. If I'm ever tried for murder, I'd sooner have her on the jury than you. She'd be less swayed by emotion. However, I didn't murder Ronald, though if somebody did . . ." She stopped. A curious expression of astonishment appeared on her face. It deepened to one of shock. Then suddenly she stood up. "But they didn't, of course. Now can I telephone for a taxi, Ruth, to take me to the station?"

"But aren't you at least going to see Edward?" Ruth asked.

"No." Leila picked up her mink jacket and slipped it on. "I've decided against it."

"But since you're here—"

"No." Leila was even more emphatic. "I don't even know why I came. It was just an odd mood I got into somehow. I don't want to see him in the least."

"But you said—"

"It doesn't matter what I said."

"Are you going back to Nigel Brooke?"

"Possibly. Now if I can telephone . . ."

"Don't bother about a taxi," Ingrid said. "I'll drive you to the station."

"No, thank you, Ingrid, I'll just ring for a taxi." Leila's voice was flat and decided.

"Well, will you at least let Edward know where you end up," Ruth pleaded with her. "That would only be kind."

"But perhaps I'm not a specially kind person," Leila answered. "And Edward and the police will hear all about my visit from you, so they can all stop worrying about me."

She walked to the window and stood there, staring out with her back to the room, until her taxi arrived about ten minutes later.

When she had gone and Ingrid had shut the front door behind her, she went back to the living room and standing in the doorway said, "We can have cold lamb for lunch and I can make a salad."

Ruth was still sitting by the gas fire with her elbows on her knees and her chin on her fists. She gazed at the hissing jets of the fire.

"D'you know, I'm sorry for Leila," she said. "Edward's never cared truly for anyone but Caroline. Leila was an infatuation which he's regretted and she knows it, poor woman. I'm not really surprised she's left him."

"Why did they come to Pottershill when he retired?" Ingrid asked. "It seems to have been disastrous for her. Why didn't they settle somewhere more exciting?"

"I suppose it was mostly the golf. And then I told them about the bungalow, because I knew from Stephanie that her friends, the Wades, were leaving. And Leila and Edward thought then that it would be just right for them."

"A funny thing—did you notice how suddenly she seemed to make up her mind not to go back to Sir Edward?" Ingrid said. "From one moment to the next her whole manner seemed to change."

"Yes, that was odd, wasn't it?" Ruth agreed. "When she arrived here, before you got in, she was asking me quite seriously—at least I thought she was serious—if I thought Edward would take her back."

"It seemed to have something to do with that talk we had about Ronald."

"Perhaps she's just in a completely muddled state of mind and hardly knows what she's doing. Now what about that cold lamb, darling? I think I must be getting better, I'm beginning to feel quite hungry."

They had lunch in the kitchen, then Ruth, who actually did not look much better, said that she thought that she would go back to bed. But first she telephoned Edward Guest to tell him of Leila's visit. Ingrid did not listen to them talking, but did the washing up and, when Ruth had gone upstairs, tried to telephone Martin again. He was still not available, but when she was asked if Sergeant Belling could help her, she said she thought that perhaps he could and when she had been put through to him, told him of Leila Guest's visit and asked him to tell Martin of it as soon as possible. Afterwards she settled down in the living room to study some leaflets, which she had picked up the morning before when she had been doing the shopping, about tours to the Caribbean.

Not that she had the slightest faith that she and Martin would get there on their honeymoon. Any money they could collect between them would be far better spent, she thought, on some special treasures for their new home. She was not even sure she really wanted a honeymoon at all. Why not spend the short leave, which was all that Martin was likely to be given, very privately, very intimately, in that home, wherever it turned out to be? The Caribbean could come later.

However, there was a certain charm now, on a rather chilly autumn afternoon, in looking at pictures of palm trees and impossibly blue seas and black-faced beauties, and in reading about the delights of drinking rum punch in the cool of the evening. Her only trouble was that while she tried to concentrate on these things, she kept hearing the voice of Leila Guest demanding if Ingrid believed that she had murdered Ronald Starkey. Did she, by any chance, believe this? Was there any sound reason why she should not at least consider the possibility? Confused by her thoughts and with the pamphlets about the Caribbean scattered around her, Ingrid drifted into sleep.

She was woken suddenly about an hour later by the ringing of the front doorbell. Because the depth of her sleep had made her lose her way in time, she thought it was morning and that the bell she had heard was her alarm clock. Then the bell rang again. By then she had recollected where she was and went to open the door.

Stephanie Legge stood on the doorstep. She was in her drooping jersey dress and her anorak and her hair hung as usual in loose strands about her face. But her face did not look as usual. It was bloated and pale. Stephanie had been crying.

"Can I come in?" she asked. "I want to talk to you. I've got to talk to someone. I simply can't stand it out there alone in the house any longer. Andrew's at the office and won't be home for hours, and even when he does come home, he won't be any use. He's never any use in a crisis. He just goes off for a round of golf and leaves everything to me. But I'm sorry, you're probably busy. I won't stay."

Stephanie looked as if she were preparing to make one of her swift flits before she had even told Ingrid why she had come.

"No, do come in, I'm not at all busy," Ingrid said. "But my mother's in bed. Shall I fetch her? She could come down if it's urgent."

"Oh no, I wouldn't dream of disturbing her." Stephanie stepped into the hall and undid the zip of her anorak. "It's really you I want to see. You can help me, if anyone can."

She dropped the anorak on a chair, pushed her hair back from her face with her fingers and strode rapidly into the living room.

Ingrid followed her and closed the door.

Stephanie made straight for the hearth rug, spun round there and faced Ingrid.

"Sandra's run away," she said.

Ingrid looked at her vacantly for a moment, then said a meaningless, "Oh?"

"You don't look surprised," Stephanie said accusingly.

"I am," Ingrid said. "Fearfully surprised." It was not true. The moment Stephanie had spoken, a vision of Sandra in the arms of the boy in the doorway of the dairy had returned to Ingrid, and with it she felt a pang of guilt because she had not troubled to warn Sandra against the boy, as Martin had suggested. "What ever made her do it?"

"It's some awful boy," Stephanie answered. "She told me all about it at breakfast. She came down early for once, fully dressed and carrying a suitcase. And she said she was going to live with this boy. His name's Gordon Smithers. I don't know where he lives or what he does. As a matter of fact, I don't believe he does anything, he just lives on the dole. It's terrible, Ingrid, I'm going out of my mind, thinking about it. I didn't know he existed. I didn't know Sandra had a boyfriend at all. We've never encouraged her in that sort of thing, she's much too young for it. But when I said so, she laughed at me and said she's been going out with him for months. Anytime Andrew's been at the office and I've been out shopping or doing some job like helping out at the Economy Centre and she's known we'd neither be home for hours, she's been out with him in his digs, wherever they are, and sometimes she's even had him in the house. Our house! And I was so certain she was a *good* girl. I knew she was lazy and selfish and inconsiderate and I did my best to correct those faults—honestly, I've been patience itself with her—but I've never known she could possibly be downright vicious. Do you know, she laughed in my face and told me this Smithers boy seduced her the very first time they met. Then—it's too awful to think about— we had a fight. Quite literally a fight. She said she was leaving and I tried to stop her and she struck me. Here." Stephanie put a fumbling hand to the side of her head.

"She really struck me and I fell over, I was so taken by surprise, and she left me lying there. I daresay she didn't really mean to hurt me, but she's such a great lump of a thing, she's much stronger than she knows. I'm fairly strong myself, but I didn't stand a chance of holding her. So I just sat there on the floor and she ran off and—" Suddenly Stephanie sat down on a chair, as if her knees would have buckled under her in another moment, and began to cry.

Ingrid stood looking at her helplessly, then asked uncertainly, "Would you like some tea?"

"Oh, no, thank you," Stephanie mumbled into her handkerchief.

"A drink, then? Whisky?"

"No, nothing, thank you, unless perhaps you've got a cigarette."

But neither Ruth nor Ingrid smoked and there were none in the house.

"Of course, I don't smoke either," Stephanie said. "That's why I haven't any of my own with me. I don't think I've smoked for ten years and I haven't wanted to, but now I suddenly feel as if I'd like a cigarette."

"Shall I pop out and buy some?" Ingrid suggested. "It'll only take me a few minutes."

"No, it would be stupid to start again, wouldn't it, when I had such trouble giving it up? I've given up so many things in my life, Ingrid, you just don't know . . . Anyway, I came here to talk to you. As I said, I felt I'd got to talk to someone. I've been there in that house all alone ever since it happened, not knowing what in the world I ought to do. I began by thinking I'd telephone Andrew, but then I thought no, they're sure to listen in on the switchboard in the office and in no time at all everyone in the place will know the whole story. And even if I rang up and said I'd been taken ill and would he please come home at once, he'd only go out and play golf as soon as he knew what the truth was. He'd never think of trying to comfort me. I make so few demands on people, they never think of me as needing comfort, but of course I do sometimes, just the same as other people. Andrew always wants to have his hand held as soon as he has the least little bit of trouble, but he never thinks I'd sometimes like it too. And he's useless at coping with Sandra. I think this is really all his fault, he's spoilt her so. Then I thought of talking to you. Yes, I thought, Ingrid, she's the right person."

"I'd like to help," Ingrid said, "but what can I do?"

Stephanie had talked herself into a kind of calm. She put her handkerchief away in her handbag.

"That fiancé of yours could find out where she's gone, couldn't he?" she said. "Then you could go and talk to her. Reason with her. You're much nearer to her in age than Andrew and I, and I think she likes you. You might be able to get her to listen to you and come home."

Ingrid thought that there was undoubtedly a record in the police station of where Gordon Smithers lived and so Martin would certainly be able to help her to find Sandra very easily, but she thought that she had already persuaded him more than was fair to search for her disappearing acquaintances. He had started a search for Leila Guest, whose disappearance had turned out not to be police business at all, he was looking for Ronald Starkey, and now Stephanie wanted him to interfere in her daughter's private life.

"You know, I don't think Sandra thinks of me as being anywhere near her in age," Ingrid said. "From seventeen to twenty-four is an enormous gap. I'm middle-aged by her standards."

Stephanie gave a wan smile. Shaking her head, she showed that she thought Ingrid's youthfulness too self-evident to need discussion.

"If you'd just try," she said. "If Inspector Rhymer could find her and you'd talk to her, I don't know, we might even get her home before Andrew gets home from the office. Then he wouldn't have to know that any of it had happened. If you put that to her, it might even mean something to her. He's so terribly fond of her. Always, always, she's been the only one who mattered to him. And she must know that, so surely she can't want to do anything so cruel to him as she's done to me."

There were tears again in Stephanie's eyes. She groped for her handkerchief.

"But that gives us hardly any time to find her," Ingrid said. "Perhaps Martin could help, but I've been trying to get in touch with him all day and he's been too busy to talk to me. I wanted to tell him that Lady Guest had been here and was quite all right—"

"*What?*" Stephanie screamed at her. She jerked forward to the edge of her chair. "That woman's been here? She's alive?"

"Yes, she came in for a little while before lunch."

Stephanie gave a strange, low wail, then began to cry with helpless violence. Her shoulders shook, tears streamed down her face and her teeth chattered. It occurred to Ingrid that this was the first time in her life that she had heard the extraordinary rattling sound of teeth actually chattering. But could Stephanie hate Leila Guest so much that she wept like this merely on hearing that she was not dead?

"Don't take any notice of me," Stephanie sobbed. "Don't worry. This is just relief. I'm crying from sheer gladness. I'm so sorry, I can't help it. I'll stop in a minute. But I'm so happy."

She abandoned herself luxuriously to her crying.

In the middle of it Ruth came in quietly and stood just inside the door, looking on. Stephanie seemed to take no notice of her.

After a moment she went on, "Isn't it dreadful, I thought he'd killed her and perhaps that Starkey man too when he found they were going away together? Andrew, I mean. He's in love with her, of course—that's to say, as much as he's capable of being in love with anyone. It wouldn't have been a really normal love, you know. He isn't much interested in sex. When we were first married I simply couldn't understand that he really didn't care for that kind of thing. It hurt me terribly. I thought when we had Sandra that it would help, but it only made things worse, because he started giving all his affection to her and I was left with nothing. And he's always liked to have affairs of a kind with other women, though it's just a sur-face sort of thing and I've never worried about it much. But he's very vain and very possessive and he can be very violent, and when Leila Guest disappeared and her dress turned up in our car, I thought—I thought—well, what else could I think? I thought he'd killed her because he couldn't stand being rejected by her and that he'd put the dress in our car just to let me know he'd done it, to tor-ture me. After all, as his wife, I couldn't give evidence against him, could I? Besides, the extraordinary thing is I still love him and I'd never have given evidence against him anyway, and he knew that. So I thought it was a way of showing me how much I was in his power, don't you see? That was the only thing that made sense. But now—now—" Stephanie blew her nose fiercely and seemed all at once to emerge from what had been almost a trance. Her voice, as she went on, was thickened by her tears, but steady. "Now you say she's alive and he isn't a murderer at all and I've been crying from sheer relief. I don't know what you must think of me."

Ruth advanced into the room and sat down, drawing her dressing-gown closely about her.

"Even if we'd all been right that Leila was dead," she said, "how could Andrew possibly have killed her? Wasn't he at the ball all the evening? Didn't you go home together?"

"Yes, but he might have left for a time in the middle, that's what I thought," Stephanie said. "He did disappear for a while. He told me he'd been in the bar, because dancing bored him, and that didn't surprise me at all, he's such a terrible dancer. But afterwards I realised what it could mean. I realised it suddenly while you were talking to Sandra, Ingrid, and that's why I came running after you to the gate and told you that lie about having left the car unlocked in the front of the Co-op. I didn't, of course. I never do. But I wanted it to have been possible for someone besides Andrew to have put the dress in the car."

"Has Andrew got a gun?" Ruth asked. "Didn't you ask yourself that?"

"For all I know, he's got one hidden somewhere," Stephanie answered. "He was in the army in the war. He'd have had a gun then and he may have kept it ever since. And the only people who could have put the dress in the car are Andrew and Sandra, and Sandra couldn't possibly have had any reason for killing Lady Guest. She hero-worships her, just because of her looks and her clothes and so on. Of course, we still don't know how the dress got into the car, but that doesn't seem important, now that we know Lady Guest's alive."

"But could Andrew ever have got into the Guests' house?" Ruth continued her questioning. "Do you think Leila would have asked him in if she'd just been going to leave with another man—even though, as a matter of fact, it happens not to have been Ronald?"

"Andrew could have got in in the easiest way," Stephanie said. "With a key. We always had a key to the bungalow when the Wades lived there, just as they had a key to ours, so that we could keep an eye on things for each other if one of us was away and so on. And when they went away they forgot it and I've kept forgetting to give it to the Guests, as of course I ought to have done, because I'm sure they wouldn't like the idea of our having it." Stephanie was beginning to sound more like her usual self. "Well, Ingrid, will you help me find Sandra if you can?"

"I'll do my best," Ingrid said.

"Thank you." Stephanie stood up. "I do realise I'm asking a lot and I realise I've made a terrible exhibition of myself. I daresay that knock on the head this morning unsettled me. I'm feeling much better now. Please forget what I've been saying. And above all, never tell Andrew a word about it. You won't, will you?"

Both Ruth and Ingrid promised that Andrew should never hear of what had just happened in that room and Ingrid saw Stephanie to the door, then returned to the living room.

"What was that knock on the head she was talking about?" Ruth asked.

Ingrid told her about Sandra's attack on her mother and her flight from the house.

"Poor Stephanie," Ruth said musingly. "I've told you, I've always wondered what went wrong with her when she was young. What I feel now is that if she'd had the courage to leave that husband of hers in time she might have turned out quite a different sort of person. But when Sandra was born I suppose she felt she had to stay. And now she and that awful girl end up brawling . . ."

Ingrid wrinkled her nose in thought. "Mother, tell me something. You know the rows Lady Guest said she and Sir Edward had about the way their whisky kept disappearing. Well, can you really imagine either of them quietly nipping away at the whisky while the other was out of the house?"

"No, I don't think I can."

"Yet when no one's around, it seems that their whisky bottles have a way of emptying themselves. And if it's impossible that their Mrs. Baldwin has been at them, doesn't it mean that somebody else has? That somebody else has been getting into the house? And if Sandra can easily lay a hand on the key, just as Mr. Legge could, and let herself in, don't you think she might be the person?"

Ruth gave one of her husky laughs. "Sandra drinking up the Guests' whisky? No, darling, that's too absurd. You'll have to do better than that."

"But if she had her boyfriend with her . . ."

"Oh, I see what you mean." Ruth thought it over. "Yes, I suppose that's just possible."

"Well, don't you think it's at least something I ought to suggest to Martin? Because it means she might somehow have been able to get at the dress, and we know she could have put it in Mrs. Legge's car."

Ruth gave Ingrid a long, rather vacant stare. It was almost as if she had not heard what she had said. Then suddenly she got up without answering and went upstairs to her room. It puzzled Ingrid.

CHAPTER 8

It was late in the afternoon when Martin telephoned
Ingrid to say that he had just heard from Jack Belling
that Leila Guest had been to the Winters' house. He was
coming straight out to them, Martin said, to hear the
whole of the story. It surprised him to discover that he
felt almost annoyed to hear that the woman was alive. It
was an anticlimax. He had been prepared to hunt for her
corpse with the greatest interest, but he felt none in Leila
Guest herself. Everything he had heard about her made
him sure he would never be able to feel any liking for her.
Not that that justified him, he recognised, in wishing her
dead. Nor did he quite go so far as actually to wish it. He
was capable of disliking some people acutely—some of his
colleagues, for instance—without wishing that one day
they would drown in their own bath water.

Nevertheless, it was a fact that the problem of Leila
Guest as a missing corpse had intrigued him, whereas the
living woman was just an annoyance. She had contrived
to carry out the fairly simple act of leaving her husband
in such a way as to cause a number of people the maxi-
mum of worry, and, from what he had heard from Jack
Belling, had not even apologised for it. Martin, tired after
a day's work of a kind that occurred all too frequently
and which seemed to be crammed with nothing but demanding and frustrating detail, arrived at the Winters'

house wishing he had never heard the damned woman's name.

It took him by surprise that Ingrid, drawing him quickly into the living room where Ruth, who had come downstairs again but was looking shivery and ill, as if her flu were gaining on her again, was roosting by the gas fire, did not immediately mention Leila Guest.

"Martin, do you remember on Monday evening we saw Sandra Legge and a boy in a doorway," Ingrid said, "and you said you knew the boy?"

He nodded. "Boy named Smithers. Worst type. I thought you might warn the girl."

"It's too late," Ingrid said. She dropped onto the sofa. "Sandra's gone off with him. Mrs. Legge was here only a little while ago, pouring it all out to us, and she wants to know if you can find the boy's address." As he sat down on the sofa beside her, she added, "Truly I'm sorry to keep bothering you with the problems of our friends."

"Friends seems to me a rather funny word for them, if you don't mind my saying so," Martin answered with a smile. "You worry about them, but I can't see any sign that you love them. Isn't one supposed to love one's friends?"

"Sometimes they're just people one's used to," she said.

"Anyway, Lady Guest's turned up safe and sound," Martin said, feeling that that matter should be dealt with before anything else. "Is there anything I ought to know about that?"

Both Ruth and Ingrid seemed to hesitate, then Ingrid said, "There are odds and ends."

She went on to tell him that Leila Guest had gone away with a nephew of May Belcher's, that she had since had second thoughts and returned to Pottershill, apparently to find out if her husband would take her back, but that suddenly she seemed to have made up her mind that she did not want to go back to him after all and had left abruptly.

"It could have been coincidence, I suppose," Ingrid went on, "that she got this mood just when I happened to mention Ronald, but I can't help feeling the things are connected and that she knows something about him. It was as if she got scared as soon as we started to talk about him."

"Didn't she know that he'd vanished?" Martin asked.

"I don't think so. But there's something else I wanted to tell you. The Guests seem to have been fighting with one another because their whisky kept disappearing, yet I honestly can't see either of them as a secret drinker, can you? So what struck me is that, just possibly, someone they don't know anything about has been getting into the house and helping himself. Is that an absurd idea?"

"It's a very interesting one," he said.

"And it's struck me too that it might be this boy Sandra's got mixed up with. What about that? He was probably out there in the neighbourhood with her quite often, and apparently the Legges have got a key to the Guests' bungalow, so Sandra could easily have let him in."

Martin nodded thoughtfully. "That means perhaps I'd better look into the girl's affairs. I'd been going to say they were nothing to do with me. She's over the age of consent and her love life isn't my business. But if there's a possibility that Smithers has been getting into the Guests' house . . ." He paused. "I don't know if it's connected with the other things that have been happening, but in any case, if you're right, it ought to be stopped."

"Martin, I wasn't going to ask you to do anything about Sandra," Ingrid said. "I only wanted the boy's address so that I could find her."

"I can find his address in the file we've got on him," Martin answered. "All the same, I think it would be best if you left this to me. If there's anything in your idea that he's been burgling the Guests' house, I'd like to talk to him, and the sooner the better."

However, as presently he returned to his car, it was a toss-up in his mind whether to go straight to see Gordon Smithers or, first, to see Edward Guest. For the girl's sake, there was something to be said for finding Smithers as soon as possible, yet if she wanted to stay with him, who was Martin to interfere? What Martin wanted, with a certain viciousness, was to get the boy under lock and key. He had been getting away with far too much. It was time for him to discover that the way of life he had chosen could have certain disadvantages. Knowing now that Leila Guest was alive, the problem of how to deal with Smithers seemed to Martin very much more important than any mysteriously mobile bloodstained dress. Yet when he started the car, he took the road towards the golf course.

The dusk was deepening as he drove. There was a tinge of purple in the little light that was left. When he got out of the car and walked up the short drive to the Guests' bungalow, there was an autumnal scent of burning leaves in the air. Someone, perhaps in the Legges' garden next door, had left a bonfire smouldering. From what he had heard of Stephanie Legge, he thought, she was just the kind of person who, while her heart was breaking, would go ferociously to work rather than sit and brood, and since she had been to the Winters' she had probably been frantically gardening.

There were lights in the Legges' windows and the Guests'. Martin rang the Guests' bell. It was answered almost at once by Edward Guest. His eyes had a tired look, but he held himself as upright as usual and was as neat and trim as always.

"Ah, Inspector," he said, "you've come to tell me that my wife's perfectly well. How very kind. I'd already heard it from Mrs. Winter, of course—indeed, she was even able to give me my wife's present address. But I appreciate your coming. As you know, I wasn't much worried about her fate myself. I saw the note she left me. But you had only my word for it that that note had ever existed, and I know you had certain suspicions of me."

He smiled. But he remained standing in the centre of the doorway, as if he had no intention of asking Martin to come in.

"It's actually about a different matter that I've come," Martin said. "I think perhaps you can help me if you can spare a few minutes."

He thought that Guest hesitated, then made up his mind to be co-operative. Standing aside, he said, "As many minutes as you like. I have singularly little to do. I'm not in the mood to mix with other people at the moment. I shrink from sympathy—or it may be, for all I know, from blame. No doubt in this affair of my wife leaving me there'll be a great deal of taking of sides. Never wise in the case of the breakup of a marriage, but people will do it. I prefer to know nothing about it."

He took Martin into the drawing room.

The curtains were drawn, there was a log fire burning in the grate and a book lying open on the sofa. The room looked comfortable and homely. It suggested contentment, not desolation. Martin thought that it would not take Edward Guest very long to get used to the absence of his wife.

"I've come to ask you a question that may strike you as a little strange," Martin said as they both sat down. "Have you ever had any suspicions that someone was getting into your house and prowling about in it when you and your wife were both out?"

"That *is* a strange question," Guest replied. "The answer is no. Now would you care to tell me why you asked it?"

"I believe your whisky's had a rather mysterious way of disappearing."

Guest gave him a startled stare. "Yes, but I told you myself that my wife . . . But that's hardly a police matter. What's on your mind, Inspector?"

"I was going to ask you if you've ever missed anything else?" Martin said.

"No, I don't think so. Oh, but wait a minute . . ." Guest paused and became very still, as if he were on the track of some elusive memory.

After a moment Martin asked, "You've thought of something?"

"Well, for some time my wife and I have kept accusing one another of mislaying things," Guest said. "All kinds of odd things. They've simply disappeared. And we've each blamed the other for carelessness. I don't think it ever occurred to either of us that someone might be coming into the house and helping himself. There were certainly never any signs of breaking in. But I wonder if you're right that that's been happening. It seems fantastic, but I suppose it's possible."

"Were they valuable things you missed?"

"No, that's why we never thought of a thief. There was no pattern in it either. Don't thieves usually specialize in some particular kind of object?"

"Usually, yes, but there can be exceptions. What have you missed?"

"A fountain pen. One or two of my shirts. Some of my

wife's nylons. She kept complaining that she always had fewer spare pairs in her drawer than she thought she had. Then, there was a bedspread that disappeared from the linen cupboard. I told her the laundry must have lost it, but she said she hadn't sent it to the laundry. Once—this will sound absurd to you—a couple of lamb chops. I remember I told my wife the butcher had blundered and given her two when she'd ordered four, but she swore there were four when she put them into the refrigerator. Oh, other things too. I can't remember them all. But never anything that you could call valuable. My wife's got some moderately good jewellery, but none of that vanished. As I said, we both believed that the things were simply being mislaid."

"But you never saw any sign that anyone had been in the house when you were out."

"No, none. We're careful about such things as seeing that the windows are closed and latched when we go out. I can't swear we never overlooked a window on any occasion whatever, of course." Guest looked at Martin frowningly. "Inspector, how serious are you about all this? You really believe this odd collection of things was stolen?"

"I think it's at least worthwhile considering the possibility," Martin answered.

"Because you've got someone in mind who may be the thief?"

"I'd sooner not answer that question at the moment. I may have more to tell you about it sometime soon. Meanwhile, may I ask you one more question? Was Mr. Starkey waiting for you here when you got home from the ball on Friday night?"

Guest looked astonished. "Good Lord, you don't connect him with these thefts—if they *are* thefts—do you? I don't say petty thieving is beyond him, but if he was going to steal anything, I think he'd be more likely to help himself to my wife's jewellery than to nylons and bedspreads."

"I didn't ask the question in connection with the thefts," Martin said. "I just wanted to tidy up a few loose ends. Lady Guest told Mrs. Winter she left him here, waiting to speak to you, when Mr. Brooke called for her."

"I don't know anything about that. He wasn't here when I got home. Have you still no news of him?"

"No."

"Did my wife know anything about why he wanted to speak to me?"

"Nothing specific."

"Are you searching for him still, or have you dropped it?"

"I'm not certain. I'm not in control of the matter. To go back to these little thefts you mentioned—"

"Always remembering," Guest put in, "that they may not have been thefts at all. My wife and I may really have mislaid the things."

"How do you mislay two lamb chops?"

Guest laughed. "That's quite a question. Couldn't you drop them into the dustbin by mistake?"

"I was going to say," Martin said, "if you think of anything more that's gone missing, will you let me know?"

"Yes, certainly. And if you have any news of my brother-in-law, will you let me know that? Perhaps I should warn you, though, that disappearing is a habit he has. And when he reappears, it may be two or three years later, his stories of what he's done in the interval are not reliable. However, I haven't really wanted to know too much. I only wish he would disappear for good, but I'm afraid that's too much to hope."

A sentiment, Martin found soon afterwards, that was

almost exactly echoed, though in more forceful language, by Ronald Starkey's other brother-in-law, Arthur Bruce, the farmer with whom Martin had already spoken on the telephone. Mr. Bruce had been visited that day by a member of the Hertfordshire police, who then telephoned Pottershill to say that Starkey, according to this brother-in-law, was a lying, cheating layabout who had never done a day's work in his life. Yet he was strangely loved by his two sisters and by a number of other women, who, to Mr. Bruce's mystification, found him charming, amusing and helpful about the house. It was a curious fact, Mr. Bruce had said, that women would put up with almost anything from a man who was helpful about the house. He could not see the point of it himself if you worked hard at your own job and brought in a reasonable income, but women were like that and Starkey knew how to exploit it. A little help with the shopping and washing-up got him a lot of tolerance and charity. It made you sick to watch him at it. If only he would disappear for good, it would be the best thing that could happen.

Martin, who by now had lost any enthusiasm he had ever had for finding Starkey, looked up the address of Gordon Smithers and made his way to it.

It was in a terrace of small, nondescript houses built of yellowish brick, with chipped stone steps leading up to doors from which most of the paint had long since flaked away. The houses further down the street had recently been demolished and a developer was moving in to erect new high-rise blocks of flats. At present there was an air of devastation about the place, almost as if it had been bombed. Down one side of the street the houses that remained were empty of occupants and had had most of their windows smashed by the youth of the neighbourhood. The house on the other side of the street, in which Smithers lived, had its windows shrouded in dingy net and an overflowing dustbin standing beside the door. As Martin approached, a black cat delicately extracted the spine of a herring from under the battered lid and made off with it.

When he pressed the bell he heard no tinkle inside the house and no one came to open the door. He used the knocker next, slamming it down hard and persistently. After a little while he heard dragging footsteps inside, the door opened a few inches and a cracked voice said, "All right, all right, no need to knock the bloody house down."

A small woman stood there, wearing tartan slippers and a tweed overcoat over a flannelette nightdress. There was a hole in one of her slippers through which a grimy toenail protruded. She had wrinkled yellow skin with a reptilian look to it and a fluff of bright ginger hair gone grey at the roots. A cigarette with an inch of ash on it was stuck to her lower lip. As she looked up at Martin the ash detached itself from the cigarette and sank to join the powdery smears on her bosom. She had a strong, unpleasant smell, even more pungent than the background smell of the house, which was compounded of unwashed milk bottles, drains, stale food and sheer mustiness.

"House is coming down anyway," she said, the cigarette wobbling on her lip. "Time too. We've got rats. Chap came here the other day, called himself a Pest Control Officer." She cackled. "Ratcatchers we used to call 'em in the days when they knew their job. This chap wouldn't do a thing himself. Said all he was supposed to do was advise me, and the chap who'd come then wouldn't do a thing without I paid him. 'Go away,' I said, 'go to hell, I'm not paying nobody for nothing in this old ruin. Going to be rehoused,' I said, 'in a nice little flat all to myself, no rats, no lodgers . . .'" She paused and gave Martin a puzzled stare, as if it had only just occurred to her to wonder what he was doing on her doorstep. "Who d'you want?" she asked. "You're police. You've got a smell I can always recognise. But I can tell you I don't know nothing. I always say to my chaps here, 'It's a free country,' I say, 'and your life's your own as long as you don't tell me nothing about it. I'm too old for worries,' I say, 'I like peace and quiet.' Where I'm going soon to my nice little flat I won't be having no rats, no lodgers, no police. Only the worms by and by. I don't hold with cremation."

She rocked with sudden laughter and some more ash fluttered down onto her bosom.

Wondering if he did indeed smell to her as strongly as she did to him, as members of different races are said to find each other's smells offensive, Martin said, "I'm looking for Gordon Smithers."

"Next floor, second door right," she said. "Can't tell you if he's in. Got a girl now. That's not illegal. I won't stand for anything illegal."

She turned and made her way along the shadowy passage into the almost total darkness at the end of it.

Martin stepped into the house, closed the door behind him and started up the stairs.

They were lit by a single dim bulb hanging from a cob-webbed flex. There was cracked linoleum on the steps and the walls were covered with paper which had once been patterned with quaint little pictures of country pubs with thatched roofs and stagecoaches at their doors, but which, apart from having been scribbled on with different-coloured pencils and lipsticks, was faded and streaked with damp. Going up, Martin wondered what Sandra Legge, moving from the spacious bungalow overlooking the golf course, was making of her new home.

He tapped on the second door on the right of the passage above.

A frightened girl's voice called out quickly, "Who's there?"

"Police," Martin answered. Then, because he thought that the name might mean something to her, he added, "Martin Rhymer."

He heard a chair moved, then footsteps, then Sandra Legge opened the door to him.

She was a terrified girl if ever he had seen one, and one of her cheeks was red and swollen, as if she had been struck there. Yet the room was not as bad as he had expected. It was tolerably clean. The furniture was cheap and rickety but at some time in the not too distant past had been given a polish. There was a single bed with a green candlewick bedspread on it. There were bright-orange curtains at the windows which looked very home-made but quite new. There was even a bunch of dahlias in a jam jar on the table.

There was also something else on the table which Martin at first took to be a fur hat, but then realised was a wig. An ash-blond wig, lying in a tumble of soft curls.

"Mind if I come in?" he asked.

Sandra backed away from him as if he were some strange and menacing animal that had escaped from a zoo and was liable to attack her. Astonishment was now mixed with her fear, yet there was an element of relief on her soft, doughy face. Her heavy body had a sagging look, as if she were near exhaustion.

"All right," she said indifferently and dropped into the only armchair in the room.

Martin came into the room, but left the door open behind him. If anyone else were to come up the stairs, he wanted to hear it.

There was a small suitcase open on the bed with a few things inside it, and a few other things in a heap on the bedspread beside it. Martin stood looking at the case.

"Packing?" he asked.

"Mm," Sandra said.

"Going home?"

"Nn."

"Going where, then?"

"Haven't made up my mind."

"It's a bad thing to set out on your travels if you haven't decided where you're going."

"It's worse thinking you know where you're going and finding you don't."

Martin recognised that there was some sense in this.

"Things didn't work out, then, with the Smithers boy," he said.

She gave him a suspicious look. "Where do you come into this? You seem to know a lot about things."

"Your mother came to see Ingrid this afternoon," he said. "She told me about what happened this morning and wanted me to help her find you. If things have gone wrong here, why don't you go home?"

"I can't."

"Why not?"

"If you can ask that, Mummy can't really have told you what happened. I knocked her down."

"She still seems to want you back. Blessed if I know why, but it's a way parents have."

She gave a stubborn little shake of her head. "I think I'll go to London."

"Using what for money?"

"Oh, I'll get some money."

"But not from Smithers." Martin sat down on an upright wooden chair. "You've been helping him, haven't you? Making this room nice for him. Those pretty curtains and that nice bedspread and those flowers too. But perhaps he's done his share, helping you get hold of some of the things. I suppose you know the Guests have missed a bedspread out of their linen cupboard. Other odds and ends too, but I won't go into that for the moment. The question is, Why don't you go home before you get into worse trouble than you're in already? Smithers didn't exactly welcome you when you turned up this morning, did he?"

Her hand went up unconsciously to the swollen patch on her cheek.

"You don't know anything about it," she said sullenly. "Not really. We had a disagreement. That doesn't mean he doesn't love me."

"All the same, you're packing."

All of a sudden her resistance crumbled. She started to pound her temples with her fists and her voice went up into a scream.

"All right, he didn't want me to come here. I've been here lots of times and we've had wonderful times together, but when I said I'd come to stay he asked me if I was mad and did I think he was going to keep me and he started to yell at me and then he hit me. And then he went out and said I'd better be gone by the time he got back. I don't understand it. I thought we loved one another. I've done all kinds of things for him, you just don't know what I've done, and I thought he felt the same about me as I do about him. But when I said that, he just laughed at me. Mr. Rhymer, I don't understand it. I don't *understand* it."

Martin spoke in the very kind tone that he could use when he wished.

"Well, yes, these things are difficult sometimes. But

you'll get hurt much worse if you stay with him than if you leave him now. I'll drive you home if you like."

"I've told you, I can't go home." Tears had begun to well out of her eyes and she smeared them away with the back of her hand. "When I heard your step on the stairs I thought perhaps it was Gordon coming back and I didn't know what he'd do to me if he found me still here. I just hoped he might have come to say he was sorry and that everything was all right. But then you knocked, so I knew it couldn't be him. He wouldn't knock. But I didn't think it could be—" She stopped abruptly, putting a fist against her mouth. "—anybody else," she muttered round it.

"Who?" Martin asked. "Are you expecting someone?"

She shrugged her plump shoulders. "Just Daddy."

"He knows where you are?"

"Yes, I phoned him from the call box in the street just before I got here. He was at home, but I asked him not to tell Mummy who was calling or where I was, because honestly I can't face her after what I did, and I said I wanted some money and he said he'd come straightaway. But when you knocked I knew it couldn't be him, because he couldn't have got here so quickly, so I was afraid it might be some friend of Gordon's if it wasn't Gordon himself. So I was scared. He's got some friends I don't like."

"You're very wise in that." Martin felt immensely relieved that he would shortly be able to hand over responsibility for this feckless child to her father. Getting up he began to stroll about the room, pausing after a moment by the table and picking up the ash-blond wig.

"D'you often wear this?"

"No, never," she said quickly. "That is—" Her fist went to her mouth again. "Only sometimes."

"Where did you get it?"

"I bought it."

"It looks expensive."

"Oh, it's just a cheap one. I bought it for fun. Gordon liked me in it."

"It wasn't a present from Gordon? He didn't by any chance—acquire it for you recently?"

Because she went suddenly pale, the bruise on her cheek stood out more lividly.

"Of course not. Where'd he get a thing like that?"

"Exactly, where?" Martin sat down again on the chair, facing her. "Sandra, wouldn't it be best if you told me the truth? You and Gordon have been getting into the Guests' house, haven't you, and helping yourselves to all sorts of little odds and ends? Nothing valuable. None of Lady Guest's jewellery, for instance. Just small luxuries, like whisky and a shirt or two and some nylons for you and a couple of lamb chops for a nice supper one evening. And of course, this wig. Lady Guest wore it at the ball with that pink Edwardian dress, didn't she?"

"No, no, no!" Sandra shrieked, her voice rising again. "It isn't true."

"Weren't you and Gordon in the Guests' house that evening?"

"No, we weren't. You're making it all up."

"But the wig's hers, isn't it? D'you realise it may even have splashes of blood on it, just like the dress?"

"How could it? I bought it."

Through the open door of the room Martin heard voices at the bottom of the stairs. One was the cracked voice of the landlady. The other he guessed was Andrew Legge's. A moment later Legge's heavy footsteps came pounding up the stairs. Sandra jumped to her feet as soon as he appeared in the doorway and threw herself into his arms.

Burying her face on his shoulder, her shrill voice came
out muffled. "Daddy, tell him to stop, tell him to go away!
He's been calling me a thief. He says I've been stealing
things from Lady Guest. You know I'd never do that. I'm
fond of her, I love her. Tell him he's a liar."

Holding her close to him, Legge looked over her head
at Martin.

"What the hell have you been doing to her?" he asked
furiously. "What are you doing here? Who are you?"

"He's police," Sandra wailed. "He's that man Ingrid's
engaged to."

"And if you want to know," Martin said, "I've been
hanging around in case the boyfriend came back before
you got here." He nodded at the girl's swollen cheek.
"Gordon isn't in the nicest possible mood today."

Legge held her a little away from him and gazed with
a kind of misery into her face. He touched her cheek
gently.

"Who did that?" he demanded. "Did this man do it?"

"No, no, no!" she sobbed. "But he's calling me a thief. It
isn't true. You know it isn't true."

Andrew Legge's small face went bloated with anger.
"How dare you?" he shouted at Martin. "If I didn't want
to get this girl home as fast as possible, I'd—I'd—" He
swallowed and seemed at a loss as to what he would do.

"According to her, she isn't going home," Martin said.
"Anyway, I'm happy to say, it's your affair now."

"Of course she's coming home."

"I can't," Sandra cried. "I can't face Mummy."

"Mummy's mad with anxiety about you," Legge said.
"We'll all forget this morning ever happened. Now get
your bag packed and come along with me."

She gave him an uncertain look as if she were trying to
make sure if he really meant it that her sins were to be

forgiven her, then she turned to the bed and started jamming her few belongings into her little case.

As she was closing it, Martin said, "Don't you want to take your wig?"

She snapped the catches of her case shut. "No."

"Then I think I'll take it," he said, "or will Gordon have any objections?"

"What's this about a wig?" Legge asked. "Is it yours, Sandra? What in hell made you get yourself a wig? You've very nice hair."

"I just thought it would be fun," she muttered. "I don't want it any more."

"I should hope not—a wig at your age, good God!" Legge picked up her case and took her by an arm. "Now come along."

They both went out of the room without looking again at Martin.

He stayed where he was until he had heard the front door bang behind them, then he picked up the wig. He was not well-informed about such matters, but he thought it was made of human hair, not any synthetic fibre, and suddenly, as the fair curls spilled over his hand, he felt intense revulsion. It was as if he were handling something dead, as in a sense he was. This hair had been shorn off someone's head and had lost its life. It would never grow any more. The feel of it between his fingers gave him the eerie sense of touching a corpse.

That this was the height of absurdity he was ready to admit. Whoever had had this hair cut from her head and sold to some wigmaker would have been paid a good price for it and no doubt would have gone straight on to grow some more to sell again. Far from being a corpse, she was probably young and vigorous. And how useful it must sometimes be, he thought, to be able to sell off portions of your body so painlessly and profitably. It was one of the less repulsive ways in which it could be turned into a financial asset.

Taking the wig with him, he went out to his car. In full darkness, punctuated only by street lamps, the neighbourhood had an even worse air of devastation than when he had arrived. Jagged, half-demolished walls jutted like broken teeth into the arch of the sky. The houses opposite, with their broken windows, had a mocking air of secrecy. Any obscenity might be concealed within them.

He drove to the police station. In the laboratory he told the one man who had not yet gone home that he would like a report on the wig. No, he did not know what he was looking for, just anything of interest, and yes, tomorrow would do. After that, Martin went to the Chinese restaurant near his lodgings, ate a not very appetising meal with a pint of beer and returned home.

Ingrid did not tell him how long she had been there, waiting for him. She was curled up in a corner of his sofa with her head buried in a cushion, half asleep. She stirred drowsily as he opened the door, then came abruptly awake, scrambled to her feet and launched herself into his arms.

She said nothing about how she had persuaded his landlady to let her into his room.

"Those people!" she exclaimed, holding on to him tightly. "Hurting one another, hating one another! I'd had all I could stand of it. I had to come here."

CHAPTER 9

It was about half past six the next morning when Martin woke, to find Ingrid already up and dressed and fumbling about in his little kitchen, making coffee.

He lay still and waited, wondering why he had ever been afraid of letting her come here. The feeling that anything out of the last sometimes desperate years could ever affect anything between them was gone like a wisp of smoke. All he had needed here to free himself of his ghosts was Ingrid herself.

He watched her as she emerged backwards from the kitchen, carrying a tray with mugs and a coffee percolator on it. She put the tray down on a chair which she pulled to his bedside, sat down on the bed and curled herself against him. He raised himself on an elbow.

"I've been a fool, haven't I?" he said. "All this waiting to have everything signed and sealed—what a waste."

It was not often that Martin admitted that he had been wrong. He was not self-assertive, but if any argument started going in a direction he did not like, he had a way of withdrawing from it. He withdrew so quietly that often it was easy not to notice that he had not budged an inch.

In the last night, however, he had budged quite a distance.

"But why get up so early?" he went on, taking the mug of coffee that Ingrid handed to him. "What's the hurry?"

"I must get home to get mother breakfast," she answered. "She often starts wandering about the house in the early hours, making tea."

"Does she know you're here?" he asked.

"I should think so. I didn't actually mention to her that I was coming, but when I went into a deep depression yesterday evening after a dose of Lady Guest and Mrs. Legge and sat brooding about what life could be like, she more or less told me you were what I needed."

"A nice woman, your mother."

"She's been in a very odd mood since yesterday," Ingrid said. "I think it started after Lady Guest came. She's got something on her mind and doesn't want to tell me what it is, as she usually does."

Martin sipped his coffee and started to collect his thoughts. An immeasurable gulf seemed to stretch between yesterday and today. The girl Sandra with her reddened, swollen cheek and her first inklings that life was not the same as her daydreams, the old hag with her smell and her powdering of cigarette ash, the squalid bed-sitting-room with the girl's pathetic attempts to make it cheerful, and the blond, curly wig, seemed all to belong to some remote time, not merely days or weeks ago, but perhaps to another age and another country. His memory seemed to have become dislocated. Although everything that had occurred in that room was clear to him, he found it almost impossible to believe that those things had happened only a few hours ago. Yet in some respects his mind seemed unusually clear.

"It's a funny thing," he observed, "but I've just remembered something I've been chasing after for the last couple of days. I told you about it. I said I was sure Guest had said something important during one of the talks I had with him, but my mind's been a blank about what it was. And now suddenly I know."

She reached out and put a hand over his mouth.

"Don't you ever talk about anything but your job, even on a morning like this?" she asked.

"But don't you want to know what I've remembered?"

"All right, go on, what is it?"

"What Guest said was that sending that dress to the Economy Centre looked as if someone wanted to draw attention to the crime."

Ingrid gave him a look of amused affection.

"What crime, Martin?"

"The murder."

"What murder? Lady Guest's alive and well. I don't think she was walking around yesterday with a bullet in her back."

"No." He smiled back at her. "No, of course not."

Her look became uneasy. "What do you mean, then?"

"Well, there's still that dress to be explained and the way it got to the Economy Centre and why it was sent there. Tell me something. Was Lady Guest wearing a wig at that ball?"

"Oh yes. I don't know what happened to it. I expect it's lying around somewhere in the Guests' bungalow."

"No, it happens to be in the hands of our scientific boys," Martin said. "I'll be interested to hear if there are splashes of blood on it."

"But where on earth did you find it?" Ingrid asked.

"In Gordon Smithers' room, when I went there yesterday evening, looking for your young friend Sandra. I caught her only just before she left. To her great surprise, Smithers had no use for her on a permanent basis. He'd told her to get out before he came back and knocked her about a bit to make his point quite clear."

"You mean Smithers took the wig and the dress too? Or did Sandra?" She shook her head. "I'm afraid I don't understand."

"Nor do I altogether, but yes, I think it was Sandra who sent the dress to the Centre. She and Smithers have made a habit of prowling about the Guests' bungalow when it was empty and helping themselves to whatever caught their fancy. Your idea that someone had been doing that was quite right. Yet they never took anything valuable. I think that must have been the girl's doing. She seems to have the rudiments of a conscience."

"Yes," Ingrid said thoughtfully. "Yes, I see. As a matter of fact, when I went to see the Legges on Sunday morning I was sure she was frightened about something. She looked as if she had something to hide."

He slipped an arm round her, pulling her down to him.

"Now that's enough of that. Suppose we talk about that flat you've fallen in love with. When do you want me to see it?"

"When can you manage it?"

"Lunchtime, if I'm lucky."

"All right, lunchtime."

They arranged to meet for sandwiches and beer in the Anchor.

Martin presently drove her home. Then he returned to his room, gave it the slight tidying up that he usually did in the mornings, made himself some breakfast and went to the police station. He was told that Superintendent Nickerson wanted to see him as soon as he got in. He started towards the Superintendent's office, then thought that before he went in he would make a quick call on the laboratory. The people there told him that the wig was a high-quality one made of European hair, unbleached, and would have been expensive. There were one or two small splashes of blood on it, of group O. Martin said that that might be useful and went on to see what the Superintendent wanted with him.

It was much as Martin had feared, though why he

should have feared it instead of welcoming it he would have found it difficult to say just then. But to withdraw from a problem when its real shape seemed just to have become apparent felt not unlike having a drug abruptly withdrawn. However, what Mr. Nickerson had to tell him was that he had been spending far too much time investigating the private lives of people who had committed no offences and that there was plenty of other work piling up for him to do.

"After all, it's not an offence to disappear without leaving an address, even if it's inconsiderate," Mr. Nickerson said. He was a burly, square-faced man with observant, restless eyes which never dwelt on anything for long. It was always difficult to decide if he was looking at you or had just found something of far greater interest somewhere behind your shoulder. "Your bloodstained ball dress remains a problem, but at least we know Lady Guest wasn't killed inside it."

"But I think I know who was, sir," Martin said, "and why."

One of Mr. Nickerson's swift glances rested briefly on Martin's face, then shot away to a corner of the ceiling, where it might be that he had seen a spider at work. He looked disapproving, whether of the spider, if there was one, and the fact that it had been allowed to survive in his office, or of Martin's statement, it would have been hard to tell.

"You want a corpse to fit the dress, do you?" he said.

"Very much, sir," Martin replied. "With blood group O."

"The commonest there is."

"Exactly."

"Go on, then. What's this all about?"

"I think we ought to start looking for the body of Ronald Starkey."

"You think Guest killed him?"

"I think it's probable."

"But I thought you'd convinced yourself he'd no motive for killing Starkey."

"He hadn't."

"I see. Yes. Well, there we are, then," Nickerson said profoundly. The spider seemed to have returned to its corner, for he was observing it again with deep concentration, thinking perhaps how easily it could spin a web compared with the blundering efforts of humans. "All right, then, get things moving. All the usual. We'll need a corpse before we can do much more. I don't want another victim walking into the middle of our investigation hale and hearty."

"Thank you, sir."

After that, Martin had a great deal to do—so much, indeed, that he nearly telephoned Ingrid to tell her that there was no hope of their meeting for lunch and going on to take a look at the flat that she had liked. He would tell her, he thought, that as it appealed to her so much she should go to the house agents and tell them that she was prepared to make an offer for the property, then she could go to a surveyor's and arrange for a survey to be made. He was willing, he would say, to leave the whole matter in her hands. But just before one o'clock he saw a short space of free time ahead of him and made for the Anchor.

He and Ingrid ate their lunch in five minutes, then drove to Mrs. Aitken's flat.

On the way Martin asked, "How's Ruth?"

"Recovering all right," Ingrid answered, but her voice was worried. "From the flu, that is. But she still seems to be in a very funny state of mind. I don't seem able to get through to her."

"Have you told her about my finding the wig?"

"Yes. Shouldn't I have done that?"

"I don't suppose it matters. What did she say about it?"

"Nothing. She just lies there, staring at nothing. The funny thing is, I've a feeling she knew about the wig already."

"That isn't impossible. She's a very shrewd woman."

"What do you mean?"

"I'll tell you sometime."

They turned into the avenue of chestnuts.

The day was doing its best to make the house at the end of the street, in its garden of lawns and tall trees, attractive. The sky was a deep, almost summery blue. The air was warm. The tawny chestnut leaves along the pavements gave off a pleasant nutty scent. October was laying on a little St. Martin's summer for them.

Mrs. Aitken came with her slow, hobbling walk to open the door for them. She held out a small claw of a hand to each of them and gave her sparkling smile. As she looked up at Martin there was the self-confidence in her air of the woman who had been a beauty.

"Do you know, you're just as I imagined you would be," she said. "I've been hoping this charming girl would bring you along soon so I could see what you were like. And I was quite right about you." Small and stooped, she was leading the way to the drawing room. "Tell me, what do you do?"

"He's a policeman," Ingrid answered for him. "He's a Detective Inspector in the Pottershill C.I.D."

"Ah, I thought it was something like that. I took one look at him and thought, a man of action. And that's just right for this girl, who thinks too much. But in work like yours, Inspector, I expect you have to use your brains too, don't you?"

"They come in useful sometimes," Martin admitted.

Mrs. Aitkin gave a little cackle of laughter. "You mustn't take any notice of the things I say," she said. "I long ago got into the habit of saying anything that comes into my head. It's one of the privileges of being very old. You don't have to worry any more about what people think of you. You can say anything you like and they keep on telling you how wonderful you are. I enjoy it very much." She gave him another dazzling smile which was almost coquettish and added, "You know, I'm ninety-two."

Ingrid forebore to remind the old woman that the last time she had stated her age she had given it as only nearly ninety. For at such an age surely you were entitled to say it was whatever you felt it to be.

"May I take Martin over the flat?" Ingrid asked. "I know my way round it by now."

"Yes, please do, and take your time." Mrs. Aitken lowered herself into her straight-backed chair. "Then come back and have a drink with me, won't you? I do so like having someone here to have a drink with."

"It would be a pleasure," Martin said, "but I'm afraid I've very little time to spare. I've got to get back into town as soon as I can."

"Ah, some important investigation," she said gravely. "I have such an admiration for the police. Their patience with those ridiculous protest marchers, when they'd far sooner be out catching criminals. My eyesight isn't very good, so I can't always see what they've got on those placards when I see them on television, but when I do manage to read one it always seems to be addressed to the half-witted. If they just put two or three exclamation marks on each placard I'm sure it would express their feelings just as well. Of course, I always watch Z *Cars* and *Softly, Softly.* Now do please go round and look at everything you want to."

Closing her eyes, she seemed prepared to drift off immediately into a little doze while Ingrid and Martin explored her flat.

About twenty minutes later they returned to the car and he drove her home.

As soon as they had started off, she said, "She's sweet, isn't she?"

"As cunning as an old serpent," Martin replied. "She's got you bewitched and knows it."

She laughed. "I wonder if you've always been so suspicious of everyone, or if it's rubbed off on you from your job. Having your trust in human beings corrupted must be one of your occupational risks, like getting your nose broken. She *is* sweet."

"She's certainly rather different from an old woman I met yesterday," Martin said. "She stank, she smothered herself in cigarette ash, she'd a dirty toenail sticking out of a hole in one of her bedroom slippers and she'd the shiftiest eyes I've seen for a long time. I'll admit that your Mrs. Aitken is a great deal more attractive."

"The people you consort with!" Ingrid said. "Where did you meet this beauty?"

"She's Gordon Smithers' landlady."

"Why bring *her* up just now?"

"Because my mind's in a very disorganized state today. This morning everything seemed crystal clear, but now it's all got muddied up. You're the trouble, my love. I oughtn't to have come out on this little jaunt with you. It's made me wish you and I were somewhere miles away together and that I needn't give a thought to dirty old landladies and young thieves and missing bodies. But that's what I've got to go back to as soon as I've dropped you."

"But what about the flat, Martin?" Ingrid asked. "You haven't said a word about it."

"Oh, I like it," he said. "I thought that was understood."

"How could I understand it if you didn't say so?"

"I'm sorry, I told you I was in a disorganized state. I really thought you saw I liked it very much indeed. I don't suppose we could possibly do better. Now I've got a suggestion. Suppose instead of taking you home I drop you off at Fordham and Knowle's and you tell them we're going to make an offer, then you go on to Gair and Loftus —they're those surveyors in Castle Street—and you ask them to do a survey and valuation as quickly as they can. Then this evening, if I can get out to see you, we'll thrash out between us just how much we can afford to offer."

Ingrid gave an excited little bounce in her seat. But a moment later her bright face clouded.

"Martin, how does one learn to keep your job out of one's life," she asked, "without keeping most of you out of it too?"

"You'll learn in time," he answered. "Doctors do it. Lawyers do it. Nurses. Even parsons. I'm sure they don't bring all the sins and the suffering of the world they work in home to tea with them every day."

"But when I think of all the horrible things that have been happening, I feel it's all wrong to have a sort of happiness getting ready to burst inside me. I know things like those won't normally come as close to us as they have this time, but I can't see myself getting used to splitting my mind in two."

"With a little practice you will."

She nodded, but looked doubtful. A few minutes later

Martin put her down at the house agents', then went on to the police station.

The search for Ronald Starkey was proceeding. However, it was not the police who found him. Only about half an hour after Martin had arrived back at the police station, the news came in that two young boys, playing in a derelict barn a little way out of the town, had found the dead body of a man, dressed in vest, pants and white socks, covered in a heap of rotting sacking. Martin, accompanied by Jack Belling, was dispatched to the barn to see if he could identify the man.

Martin's previous attitude to Ruth's lodger had been wholly impersonal. He started off for the barn without being aware of feeling any particular emotion. Yet as the smell of death met him and when he saw what the rats in the barn had left of Ronald Starkey's sly ingratiating face, he wondered how he had ever had the confidence to tell Ingrid that a little practice would teach her how to split her mind in two.

When he returned to the police station there was a message waiting for him from Ingrid, asking him urgently to call her as soon as he got in. When he did so, her answer came in a high, unusually shrill voice.

"Martin, she's gone. Sometime while we were looking at the flat, or I was talking to the man at Fordham's or the surveyor, she took the car and went. And I'm scared, Martin. I'm sure she knows something more than she's been telling us. But where's she gone and why?"

"I think she's gone to see Guest," he said. "I think I know what she's up to. But I thought she was too ill to go out. I thought she might telephone and I didn't see what harm that could really do, but I never thought of her going walking into trouble herself. All right, Ingrid, try not to worry. I'll get out there as quickly as I can."

CHAPTER 10

As Ingrid had told Martin, she had left Ruth lying in bed, staring at nothing. Ingrid had left a lunch tray beside Ruth's bed, which for some time Ruth ignored, as she was ignoring the collection of thrillers that Ingrid had brought from the library that morning. Ruth was feeling rather worse than she had felt yesterday before Leila Guest's visit. The reason, she knew, was emotional. Her flu was not really any worse. Her temperature was almost down to normal and her catarrh was abating. But her limbs ached and she felt a heavy pounding in her head, and the thoughts that chased each other through her mind were enough to make anyone feel ill.

After a while she poked at the cooling scrambled egg on her tray, ate a little of it and drank the lukewarm coffee. Then she returned for a time to commune with her own thoughts. She had done so much thinking during these few days of lying here feverish, had suffered from so many dark and difficult fears, that she had not much trust in the validity of any of them. Nevertheless, certain things seemed to her self-evident, and if she did nothing about them she knew that she was liable to regret it for the rest of her life.

She thought of telephoning. But a telephone conversation is a very chancey affair. It may go just as you intend; on the other hand, it can so easily go wrong. It can be cut off abruptly before you have said half of what you

want to say. You cannot watch the expression on the
other person's face while you are talking. You cannot tell
what effect you are having. But the thought of getting up
and getting dressed was extremely unattractive. She let a
little more time pass before at last throwing back the bed-
clothes and swinging her feet down to the floor.

She felt shivery, so she dressed in a warm trouser suit
with a thick polo-necked sweater inside it and put on her
sheepskin jacket. Going out to the Mini, which as usual
was parked beside Ronald Starkey's Vauxhall, she felt a
little lightheaded. She felt glad that the day was fine and
that she would not have to cope with the hypnotic swaying of windscreen wipers or the sudden battering at the
little car of heavy gusts of wind. In fact, after a few minutes of driving, she began to feel almost glad that she had
come out. The sunshine seemed to be giving her strength.
The air of the mild, still afternoon seemed to have cleared
her clogged nostrils. She had been a fool, she thought, to
have allowed herself to be persuaded to stay in bed for so
long.

Yesterday, she realised, she had taken to her bed, after
Martin's visit, as a refuge. It was the one place where she
could inconspicuously think her own thoughts and at
times, when she could not bear them, practically blot
them out by burrowing into her pillows. But you could
not go on doing that kind of thing indefinitely, and since
her talk with Ingrid this morning she had known that she
had not much time left. She understood what the discovery of the wig was sure to mean to Martin, even if Ingrid
did not.

Edward Guest opened the door to her. He looked startled at seeing her, but was about to give her his usual
friendly kiss when she withdrew sharply.

"Don't," she said, "I'm still infectious. I oughtn't to

have come, but there are some things I've got to say to you."

"My dear, you look a wreck." He closed the door behind her as she stepped into the hall and took her to the drawing room.

The room had subtly altered since Ruth had seen it last. There were books lying about. The piano lid was open, as if Edward had been trying his hand at playing it. Some letters had accumulated on the coffee table instead of having been neatly sorted out on the writing table. The cushions were dented.

There were other small changes that Ruth did not analyse, but which amounted to the fact that there was a faint gloss of untidiness everywhere. It surprised her. She had always thought that it was Edward as much as Leila who had had the passion for perfection that this room had always expressed to her.

Edward saw Ruth's glance go to the piano and smiled.

"Yes, I've been strumming," he said. "Terrible noise, but there was no one here to hear me. It's a funny thing, Caroline was really musical, she had a lot of talent, yet she didn't mind it when I bashed away at her beloved piano for my own amusement. And Leila can hardly tell one note from another, yet she nearly screamed if I touched it. I always thought the piano was one of the things I might take up when I retired, you know. I even thought I might take some lessons. But Leila told me I was mad. Perhaps I was. Now sit down and let me get you a whisky. You look as if you need it."

Ruth was glad to drop into a chair. She looked at him wonderingly.

"Edward, do you honestly not realise that the police are going to be along anytime now to arrest you for murder?" she asked.

He looked perplexed.

"Murder?" he said. "But good Lord, Ruth, you saw Leila yourself yesterday. You rang me up to tell me so." He gave her a thoughtful look, as if he were wondering how much fever might have disordered her brain. "You remember doing that, don't you? Now what about some whisky?"

"Yes, yes, some whisky would be very nice, thank you, but I'm not delirious," she said, "so do hurry up and come and sit down so that we can talk and not waste time. We may not have very much. And I came on purpose to warn you."

"That was very kind of you, my dear," he said, "and I'm very grateful to you, but as I said to you, Leila—"

"Not Leila," she interrupted impatiently. "Ronald. I'm sure Martin's got round to realising that you murdered Ronald, and he's got a lot of evidence to support it, and I know the police will be here soon, so I thought I ought to come and explain the whole thing to you. Then you can think out your situation and not be taken by surprise. Because I think you may find things more difficult than you expect."

"Ronald?" he said. "Well, of course that's different."

He turned towards the drinks tray and poured out two drinks, making them both very strong. He put one glass into Ruth's hand and took a quick drink from the other.

Then he asked, "Would you care for some aspirins too? The house is well supplied with all the necessities of life."

"Edward, please be serious," she said earnestly. "You won't find it any fun being tried for murder."

"There aren't so very many things that I find fun nowadays," he said. He sat down facing her across the hearth, hitching up his neatly pressed trousers, crossing his legs and taking another gulp of his drink. "I thought I'd persuaded that future son-in-law of yours that I'd no motive of any kind for murdering Ronald. He seemed to accept the fact that Ronald's attempt to blackmail me hadn't scared me at all."

"Oh, he did," Ruth said. "He doesn't think you intended to murder Ronald. He knows you mistook him for Leila."

"Now, how in the world could anyone do that?"

"Quite easily, if he was dressed up in your mother's ball dress and Leila's wig."

"That wig!" he exclaimed. "I wonder what happened to it. I can't remember seeing it anywhere."

"It's turned up in the lodgings of Sandra Legge's boyfriend. It was a silly mistake of Sandra's to keep it instead of sending it to the Economy Centre with the dress, but apparently she couldn't resist it, and I should think it'll prove that she and the boy were in here on the night of the murder."

"So that's what Rhymer was thinking of when he questioned me about some minor thefts we've been having—so minor we were never quite convinced they could really be thefts. It was Sandra and her boyfriend, was it? But how have they been getting in? We were always reasonably careful about locking up when we went out and we never saw any signs of anyone breaking into the house."

"They got in with a key that the Wades forgot and left behind with the Legges when they went off to Australia. The Wades, the people who lived here before you, were great friends of the Legges and they used to do all sorts of odd jobs for one another and they'd got keys to each other's houses. So the Wades' key has been lying about in the Legges' house for the past year. Stephanie told us so."

"But even if that girl was in here on Friday evening, what made her send the dress to the Economy Centre?"

Edward asked. "Because I suppose that's what you mean she did."

"Well, Ronald brought Leila home from the ball, didn't he, and when that man Brooke collected her she left Ronald here, waiting for you. She left that note for you, telling you she was leaving you, and she left the pink dress and the wig thrown down somewhere, I suppose in your bedroom. And when Ronald had sat around for a while, doing nothing, he got bored and he thought he'd dress up in those things—"

"Wait a minute. Why ever should he have done that? Was he a transvestite?"

"It wouldn't surprise me. He'd got a good many quirks and he did insist on going to the ball dressed up as a girl. But mainly I think it was just his idea of humour. He thought it would be amusing to give you a shock. I suppose he thought you'd be amused too, or he wouldn't have risked doing it, because he was hoping, so Leila thought, to get some money out of you. And when he'd just got dressed up you came in and found the note Leila'd left for you and while you were reading it I imagine you must have heard a noise from the bedroom and thought Leila hadn't gone yet, and you went and got that gun of yours and went into the bedroom and there was Leila with her back to you, standing in front of the mirror. And you shot her. Only, of course, it was Ronald."

Edward gravely stroked his jaw. "Does Rhymer believe all this?"

"I'm afraid so. Ever since he found the wig and realised how easily Ronald could have disguised himself as Leila. Of course, I've known all along there must be a wig somewhere, because someone who's such a perfectionist about her clothes as Leila would never have worn an Edwardian dress with her own short hair, and I've had a suspicion of what happened ever since she turned up alive. I think she realised it too as soon as she heard Ronald was missing. She guessed you'd tried to kill her. Anyway, she quite suddenly dropped any idea of coming back to you and left us as quickly as she could."

"I see. But you still haven't explained what happened to the dress."

"Well, after you'd had the shock of finding you'd killed the wrong person," Ruth said, "naturally you began to wonder what you ought to do with him. And first of all you took off the dress and the wig and put his body into his car, which was parked somewhere near, perhaps in the road, where you didn't notice it when you first arrived, and you put the doll and the dress he'd borrowed from Ingrid into the car too, then you drove off, I don't know where, and dumped him. Then you drove his car to my house and left it outside in its usual place, so that it would look as if he'd driven back himself, and then you walked home. You'd have been planning meanwhile how to get rid of the bloodstained ball dress which you'd left lying in the bedroom, but when you got home it was gone, and that must have been a very nasty discovery. You'd have been utterly bewildered, and more bewildered still when you heard from Ingrid next day that the dress had turned up at the Economy Centre."

"Bewildered, in such circumstances," Edward said, "would be a beautiful understatement. But what do you suppose had happened?"

"There's no need to pretend, Edward," Ruth said. "You know I'm telling the truth. And I'm only here to help, not to make trouble for you. What had happened is that Sandra and Gordon Smithers, seeing the house dark and supposing that none of you had got back from the ball yet, thought they'd have a prowl around and let themselves in to see if there was anything worth picking up. And of course they found the dress and the wig. And they deduced from the bloodstains that you'd murdered Leila and were out disposing of the body, and Sandra, who was very attached to her, wanted you caught. But the two of them didn't want it known that they'd been in the house, so they took the dress and the wig away with them and Sandra slipped the dress in with Leila's other things in her mother's car, so that it would be spotted next day at the Centre and get an inquiry started. Just as it did. Quite clever of her really. I shouldn't have thought she had it in her. But the silly girl couldn't resist keeping the wig for herself, and Martin found it yesterday."

"I see, I see. But you're a bit short on proof, aren't you, my dear?"

"Don't you think that when the police put pressure on Sandra she'll tell them all about that evening?"

Ruth put her glass down. She had not yet touched the whisky. She still had a lightheaded feeling and was afraid that the drink might make it worse.

"Have you still got the gun, Edward?"

He did not answer, but got up quickly and went out of the room.

He came back almost at once, holding a gun. Ruth had no idea what kind it was. It was small, but looked very deadly. Edward stood in the middle of the room, frowning down at it with concentration, shifting his grip on it slightly, as if he were trying to find the one that felt best.

"Do put it down," Ruth said. "You look so threatening."

A look of grim amusement appeared on his dark, handsome face.

"Are you afraid I might turn it on you, Ruth?"

"My dear Edward! As if I'd have come if I'd been afraid of that."

"You know, I've owned this thing for years," he said.

"All those years in Tondolo, when there was always some sort of political trouble, almost on the edge of civil war sometimes, and I never had to use it. Why aren't you afraid?"

"For one thing, you've been my friend for thirty years. You wouldn't change your feelings about me all in a moment."

"Yet that very thing can happen. Some people turn into raving maniacs all in a moment." He gave an abrupt sigh, laid the gun down on a table and sat down again. "Yes, I was a maniac for a short time on Friday night, and when you've been over the edge of madness even for a short time once in your life, you haven't much confidence that it couldn't come over you again. Sometimes I think I'm not really sane, Ruth. I don't think I have been since Caroline died."

Ruth watched him as he tipped the whisky this way and that in his glass, watching it with an almost dreamy stare.

"Really, Caroline was the reason why you had that mad impulse to shoot Leila, wasn't it?" she said.

"Oh yes," he said. "I never forgave Leila for tempting me into infidelity to Caroline just when she needed me most. There's at least a little grain of truth in that, even if it isn't the whole story. I was never fair to Leila, any more than I was to Caroline. That's shabby, isn't it? But I think the real trouble with Leila was that she bored me so. She's a very dull woman. After Caroline, with all her talents that she never quite learnt how to use, and her sudden frantic enthusiasms and her appalling depressions, it felt like living in a dead-flat countryside when you've been used to mountains and streams. I was quite the wrong person for Caroline to have married, of course. She ought to have married an artist or an actor or someone who could have given her an adventurous life. I was staid and ambitious and I wanted her to dedicate herself to my career. She was terribly wasted. I think it was realising that that made me tolerate Ronald even as much as I did. He was a wasted person too, with a lot of talents gone to seed because he was so crooked. Caroline wasn't crooked, though she could lose herself in fantasy, just as Ronald could. They were similar in a lot of ways. Whenever I saw him I used to think that there, but for the grace of God, went Caroline. However, I did fall violently in love with Leila for a time, and the worst possible time for Caroline. Don't imagine I don't blame myself."

Edward's voice had become quiet and level, almost as if he were talking to himself. He did not look up at Ruth, but went on watching his gently swirling whisky.

"I think the main reason why I tried to shoot Leila," he said, "was the discovery that I'd failed Caroline so terribly for the sake of someone so tawdry, who didn't love me at all. Perhaps never had. When I saw her note and then, as I thought, heard her moving in the bedroom, I decided to shoot her and then shoot myself. I haven't found life specially worth living recently. So I thought I'd settle everything. It seemed to me just as good an idea to shoot myself as to wait for a stroke or a heart attack. Then when I'd shot Leila, as I thought, it turned out to be Ronald, and I was damned if I was going to shoot myself for Ronald. I decided I was going to try to get away with it." At last he looked up at Ruth. "Wouldn't you have done the same?"

"Well, I expect if I ever shoot anyone I'll try to get away with it," she said.

"But you find the initial action difficult to imagine." He gave a brief laugh. "Yes, I did just as you said. I took the wig and dress off him and put him in his car and drove out into the country and hid him in the corner of an old barn I'd noticed some time or other and covered him in some old sacks and hoped no one would find him till he was unrecognisable. Then I drove his car back to your house and walked home, meaning to choose a suitable time for burning the dress and the wig. And they'd vanished. I simply couldn't believe it. I went on walking from room to room as if I thought they could have got up and moved themselves. I even wondered if I could have deluded myself that I'd stripped Ronald and had really hidden him in the barn still in his fancy dress. I knew I hadn't, but it took me a while to face the fact that some-one had been in the house while I'd been gone and had taken the things away. It seemed utterly mad. Of course, I expected blackmail. I thought someone must have watched the whole thing through a chink in the curtains and I began to ask myself what I'd do when it started. I've always felt very complacently that I'd never give in to blackmail, but then I'd never done anything before that could give anyone power over me. And I began to wonder who it would turn out to be. And then, of all fantastic things, Ingrid appeared next day and told me that ex-traordinary story about the dress having turned up at the Economy Centre."

He finished his whisky quickly, got up and refilled his glass.

"I don't think she realised how difficult I was finding it, all the time she was here, not to laugh and laugh," he went on. "I know I behaved rather oddly and she noticed it. For one thing, I was slightly drunk. Waiting for the tel-ephone to ring and for some threatening voice to tell me how many thousands of pounds I'd got to pay for silence, I'd been drinking steadily. After her visit I began to sober up. Then Rhymer came next day, but it seemed to be Leila he was looking for, so I wasn't much worried. I knew she'd turn up again sooner or later. And as time H 29 passed I began to realise how little I missed her. In fact,

I've been finding life a good deal more comfortable without her than it ever was with her. I've been letting the place get untidy if I felt like it, I've been playing the piano, I've been thinking I might take a long cruise on some kind of small cargo ship. I like the sea, but not in one of those floating hotels, which were the only kind of thing that would ever have interested Leila. Oh, the last two or three days have really been very pleasant and I'd nearly stopped feeling scared until you came. Ruth, why *did* you come? You said you'd come to help me, but don't tell me you sympathise with a murderer."

She picked up her glass at last and drank a little.

"I've known you for more than half my life," she said. "You were very good to me when I needed you. I couldn't sit back and do nothing."

"So you thought you'd give me the chance of bolting off into the blue, taking refuge in South America if I could get there, or shooting myself rather than let myself be arrested. That was very kind." There was irony in his voice. "As a matter of fact, I'd given the matter a good deal of consideration before you came and I'd decided that if it came to the point, I'd give myself up. I don't expect to survive prison life very long and for a little while I may even find it interesting. It feels agreeable in a way to abandon all responsibility. I'm withdrawing from the battle of life, one of the badly vanquished. And I really don't seem to mind it so very much. So cheer up, my dear. I think I'll play the piano for a little, if you can bear it. It'll help to steady my nerves before the police get here."

Ten minutes later, when Martin and two constables arrived and Ruth, white-faced, let them into the house, Edward Guest was seated at the piano, playing a Chopin Étude with an appalling lack of skill but a look of rapt serenity.

006544481

Ferrars   c.1
    The pretty pink shroud.